FAR OUT
FOLKTALES

STONE ARCH BOOKS
a capstone imprint

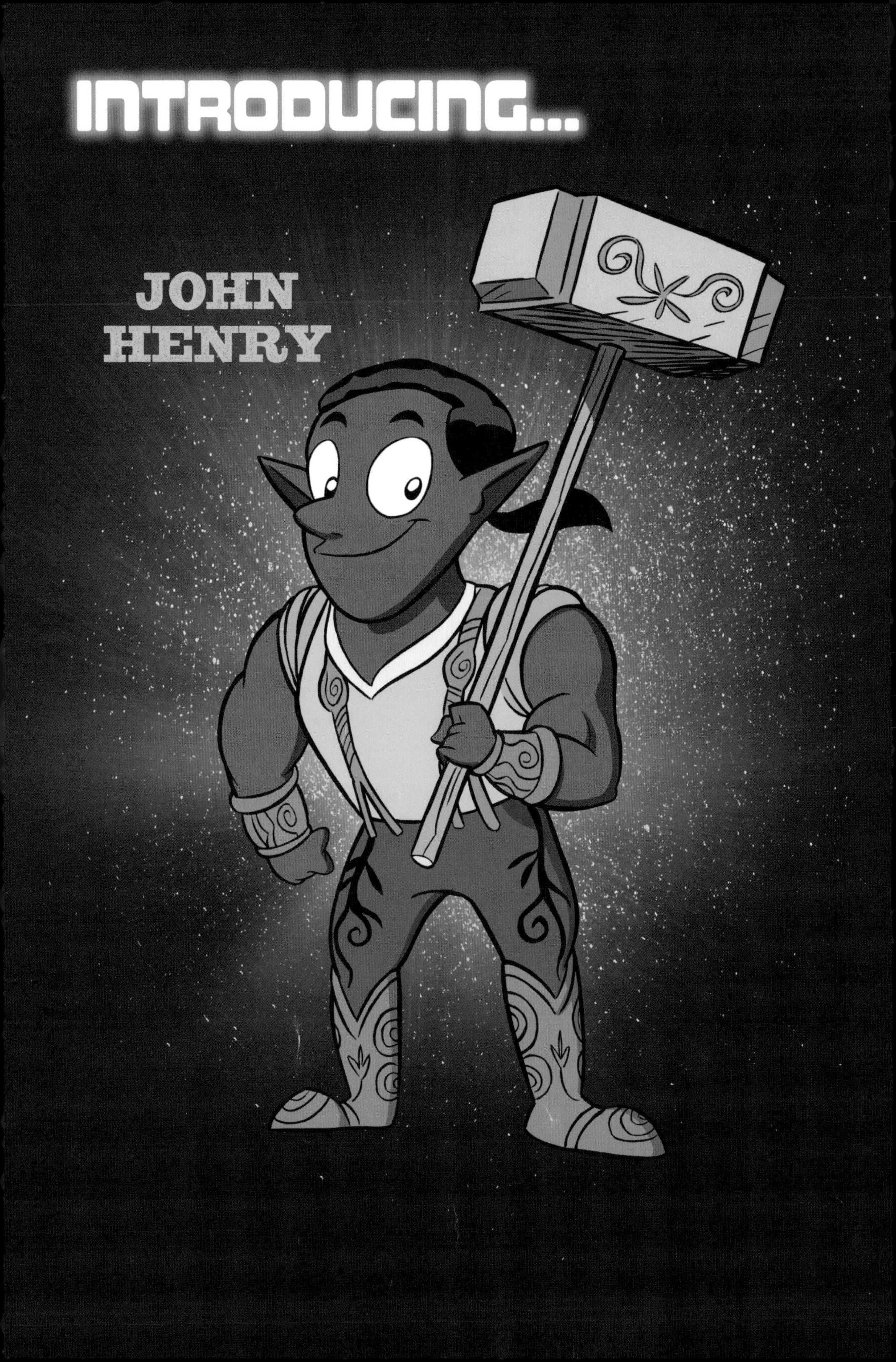
INTRODUCING...
JOHN HENRY

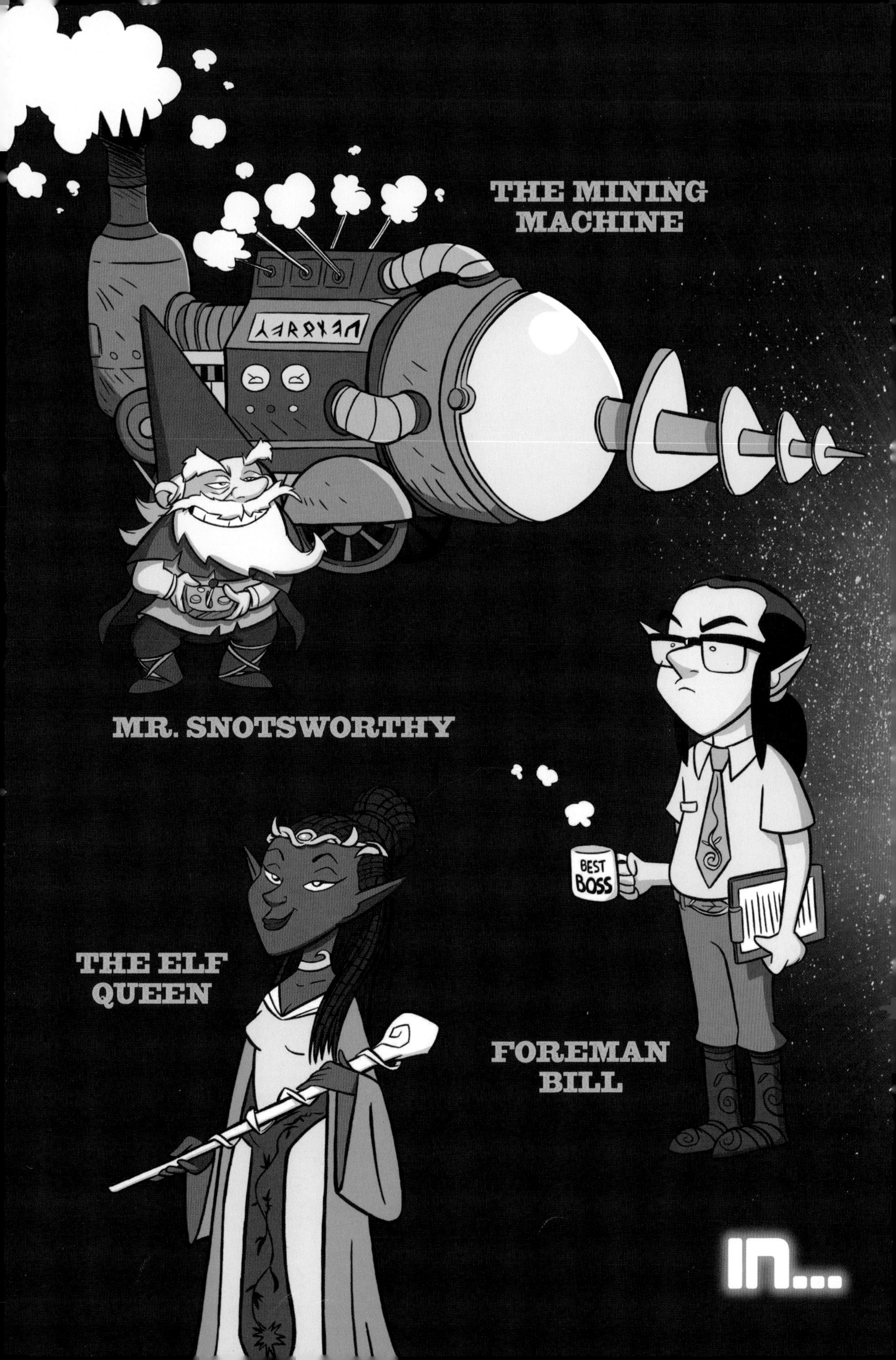
THE MINING MACHINE
MR. SNOTSWORTHY
BEST BOSS
THE ELF QUEEN
FOREMAN BILL
IN...

Far Out Folktales is published by
Stone Arch Books
A Capstone Imprint
1710 Roe Crest Drive
North Mankato, Minnesota 56003
www.mycapstone.com

Cataloging-in-Publication Data is
available at the Library of Congress
website.
ISBN 978-1-4965-7844-0 (hardcover)
ISBN 978-1-4965-8009-2 (paperback)
ISBN 978-1-4965-7849-5 (eBook PDF)

Designed by Brann Garvey
Edited by Abby Huff
Lettered by Jaymes Reed

Printed and bound in the USA.
PA49

Summary: There's no stronger elf in Gem
Forest than John Henry. With a swing
of his hammer, he can carve a perfect
mining tunnel. So when a gnome says he
has a machine that digs better than any
miner, John Henry is ready to prove him
wrong. But as the contest begins, the
device shakes the mountain—and awakens
angry orcs! Can John Henry defeat the
creatures and the gnome's contraption?

FAR OUT FOLKTALES

JOHN HENRY, STEEL-DRIVIN' ELF

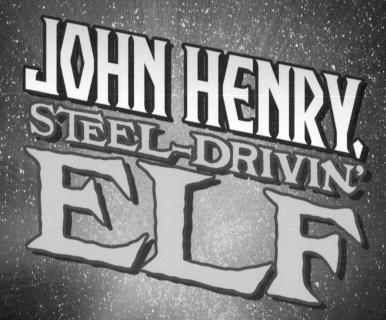

A GRAPHIC NOVEL

by Benjamin Harper
illustrated by Alex Lopez

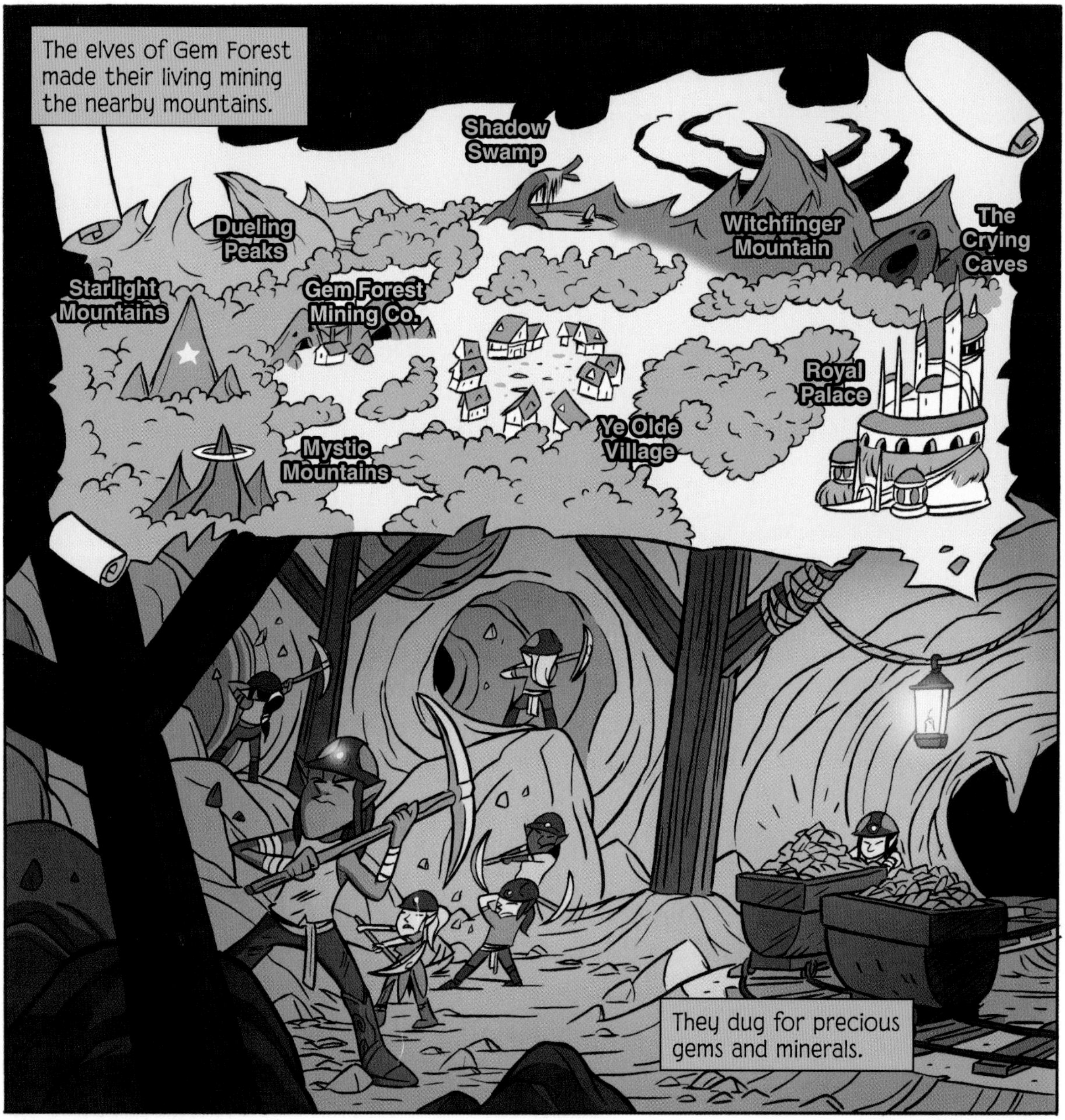
The elves of Gem Forest made their living mining the nearby mountains.
Shadow Swamp
Dueling Peaks
Witchfinger Mountain
The Crying Caves
Starlight Mountains
Gem Forest Mining Co.
Royal Palace
Ye Olde Village
Mystic Mountains
They dug for precious gems and minerals.

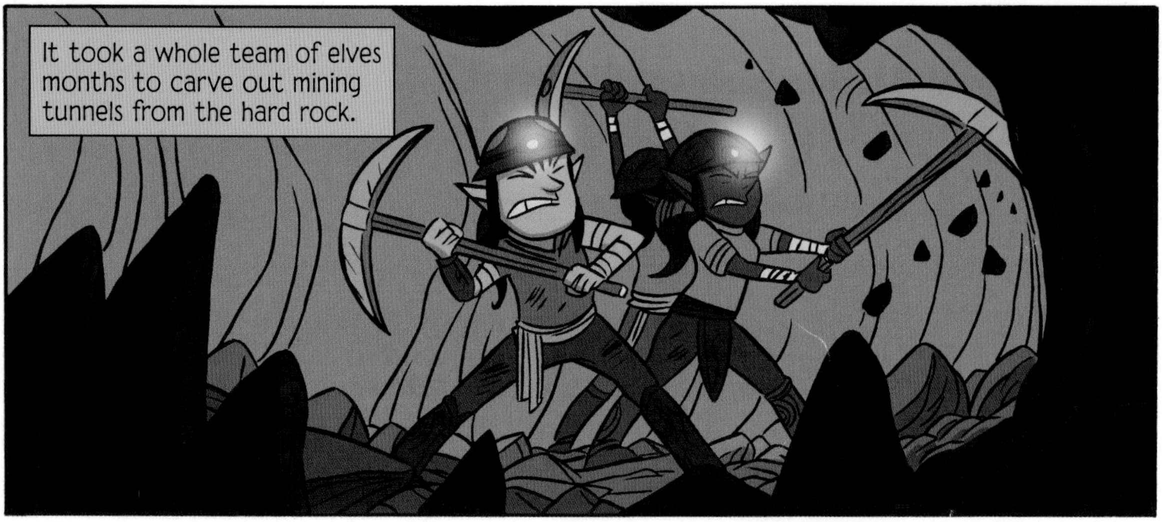
It took a whole team of elves months to carve out mining tunnels from the hard rock.

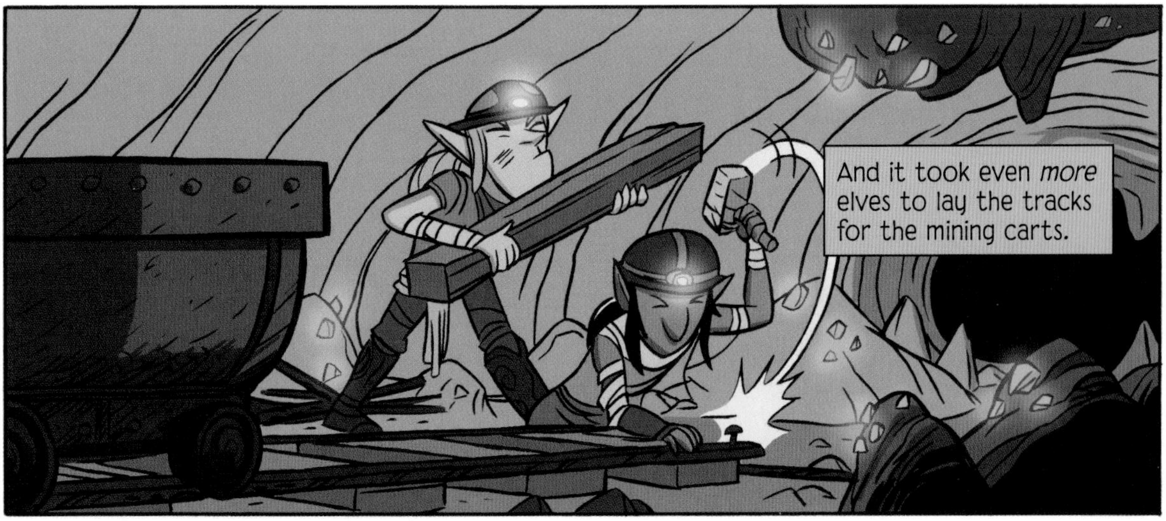
And it took even *more* elves to lay the tracks for the mining carts.

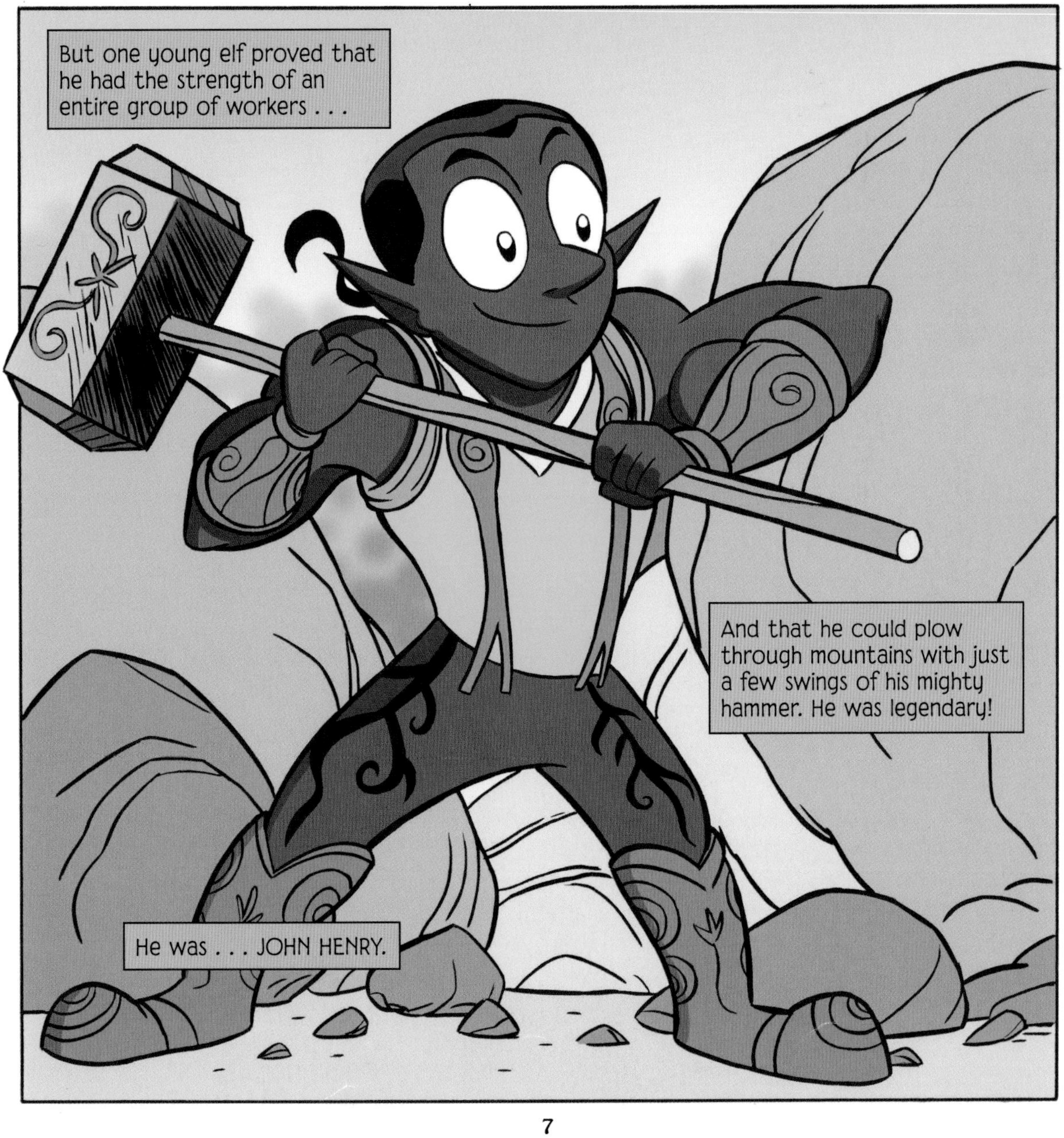
But one young elf proved that he had the strength of an entire group of workers . . .
And that he could plow through mountains with just a few swings of his mighty hammer. He was legendary!
He was . . . JOHN HENRY.

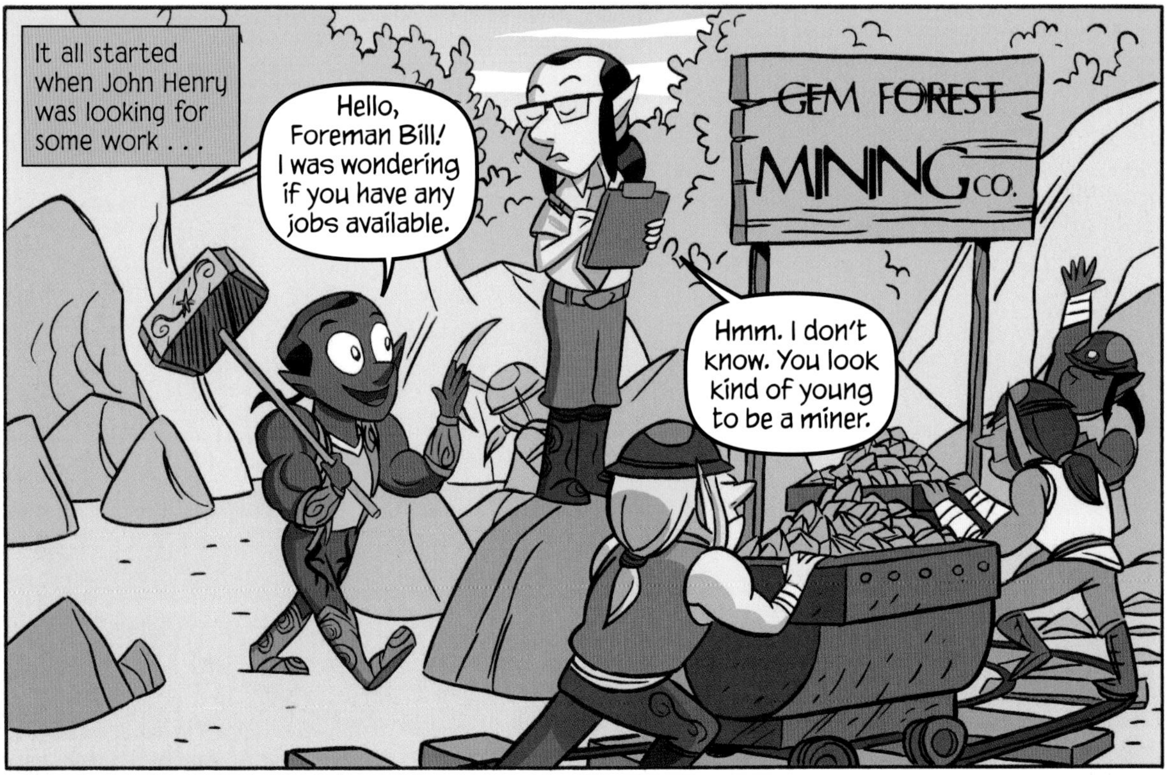
It all started when John Henry was looking for some work . . .
Hello, Foreman Bill! I was wondering if you have any jobs available.
GEM FOREST MINING CO.
Hmm. I don't know. You look kind of young to be a miner.

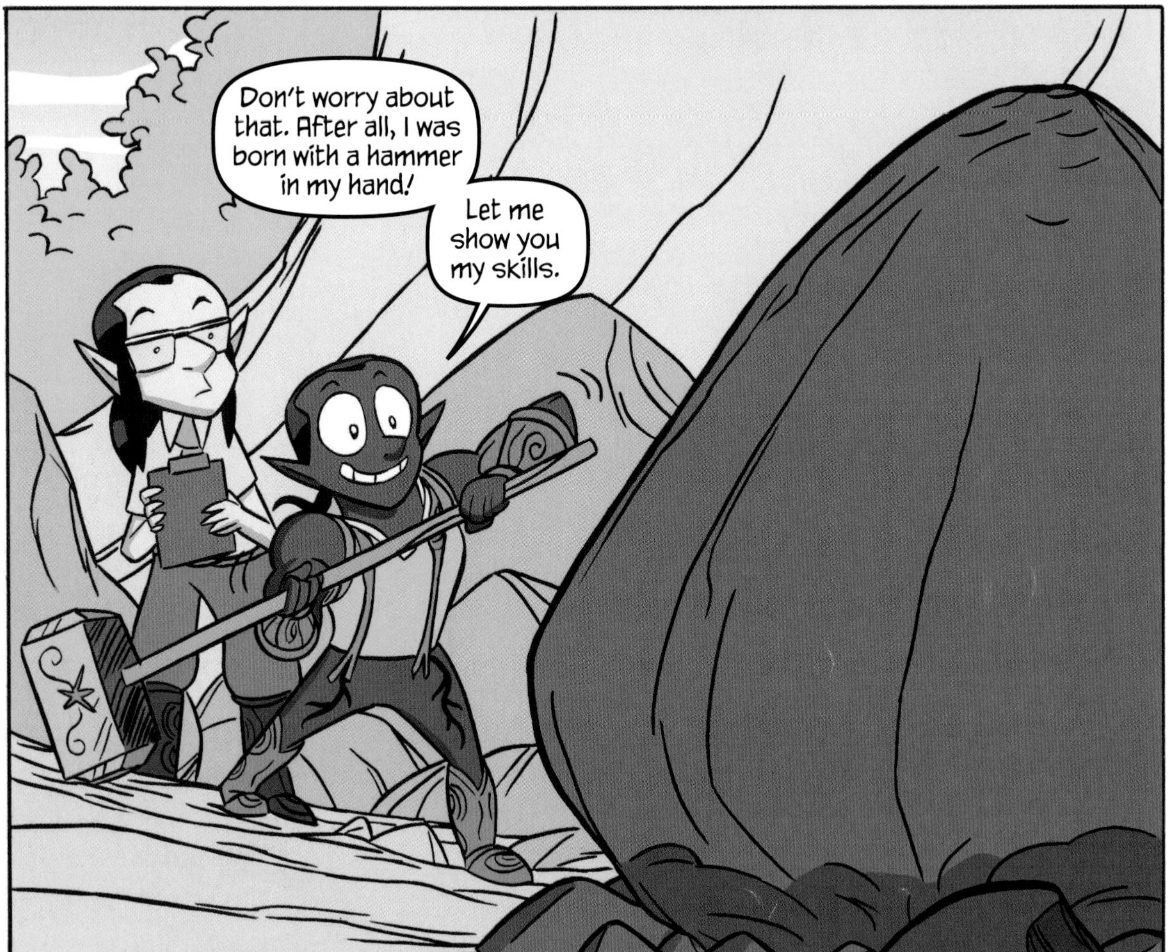
Don't worry about that. After all, I was born with a hammer in my hand!
Let me show you my skills.

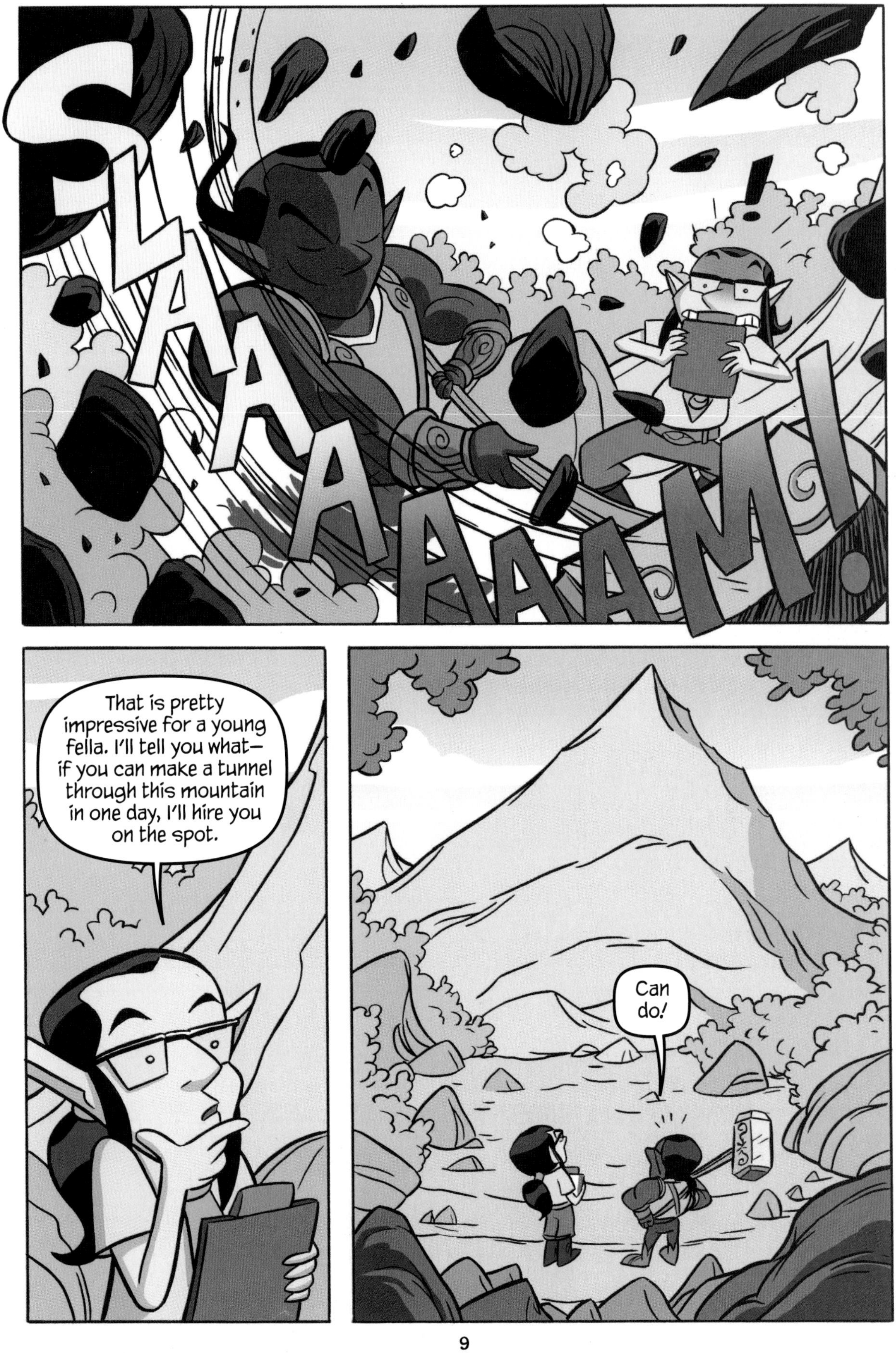
SLAAAAAAM!
!
That is pretty impressive for a young fella. I'll tell you what— if you can make a tunnel through this mountain in one day, I'll hire you on the spot.
Can do!

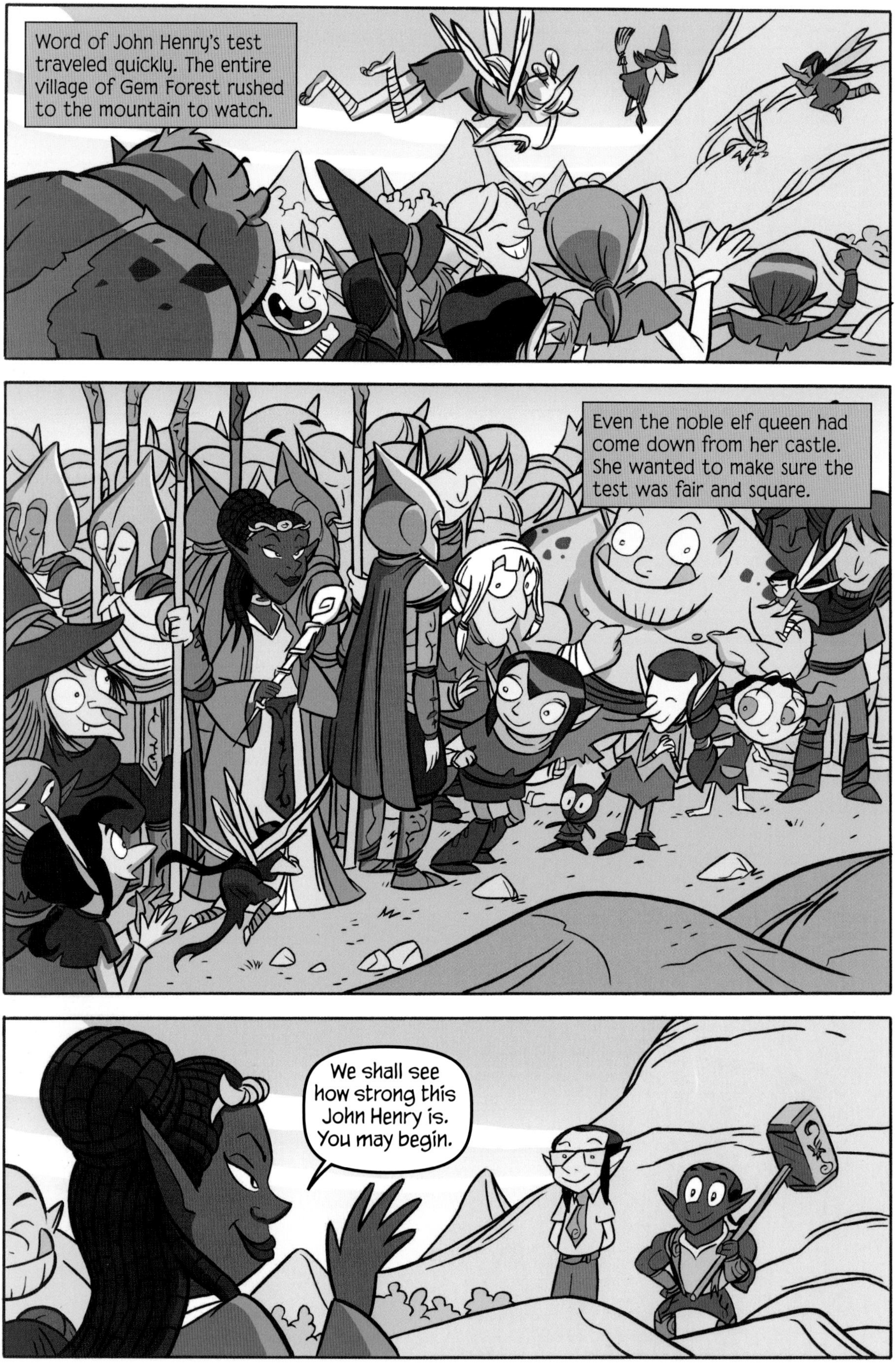

Word of John Henry's test traveled quickly. The entire village of Gem Forest rushed to the mountain to watch.
Even the noble elf queen had come down from her castle. She wanted to make sure the test was fair and square.
We shall see how strong this John Henry is. You may begin.

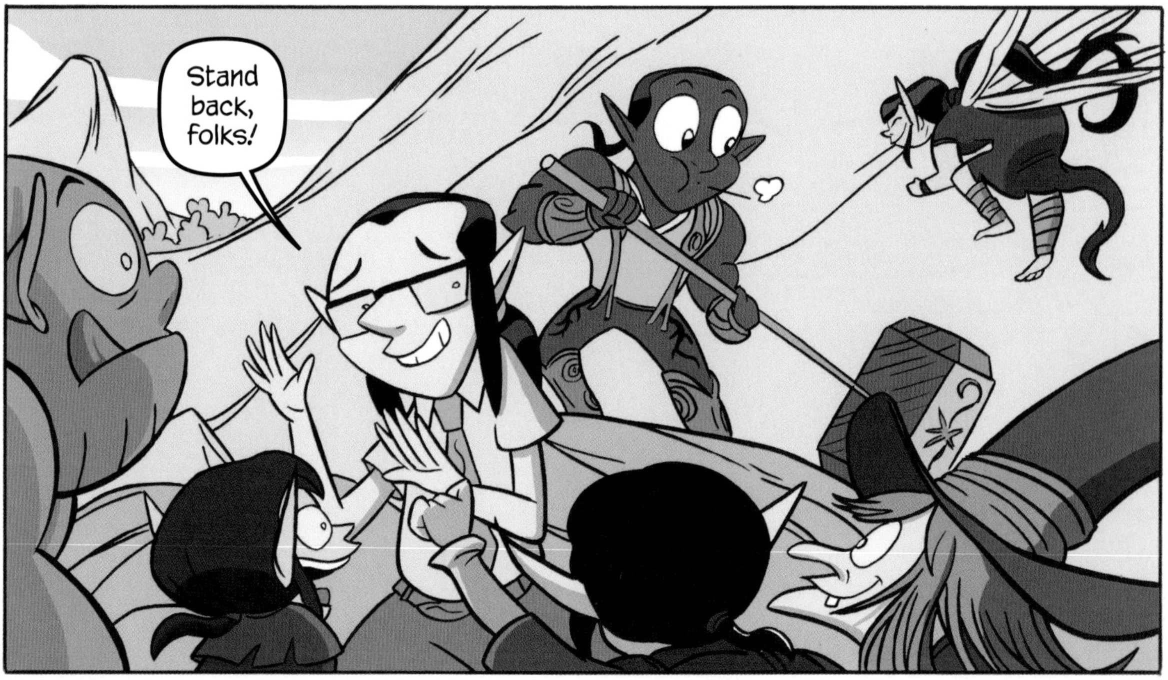
Stand back, folks!

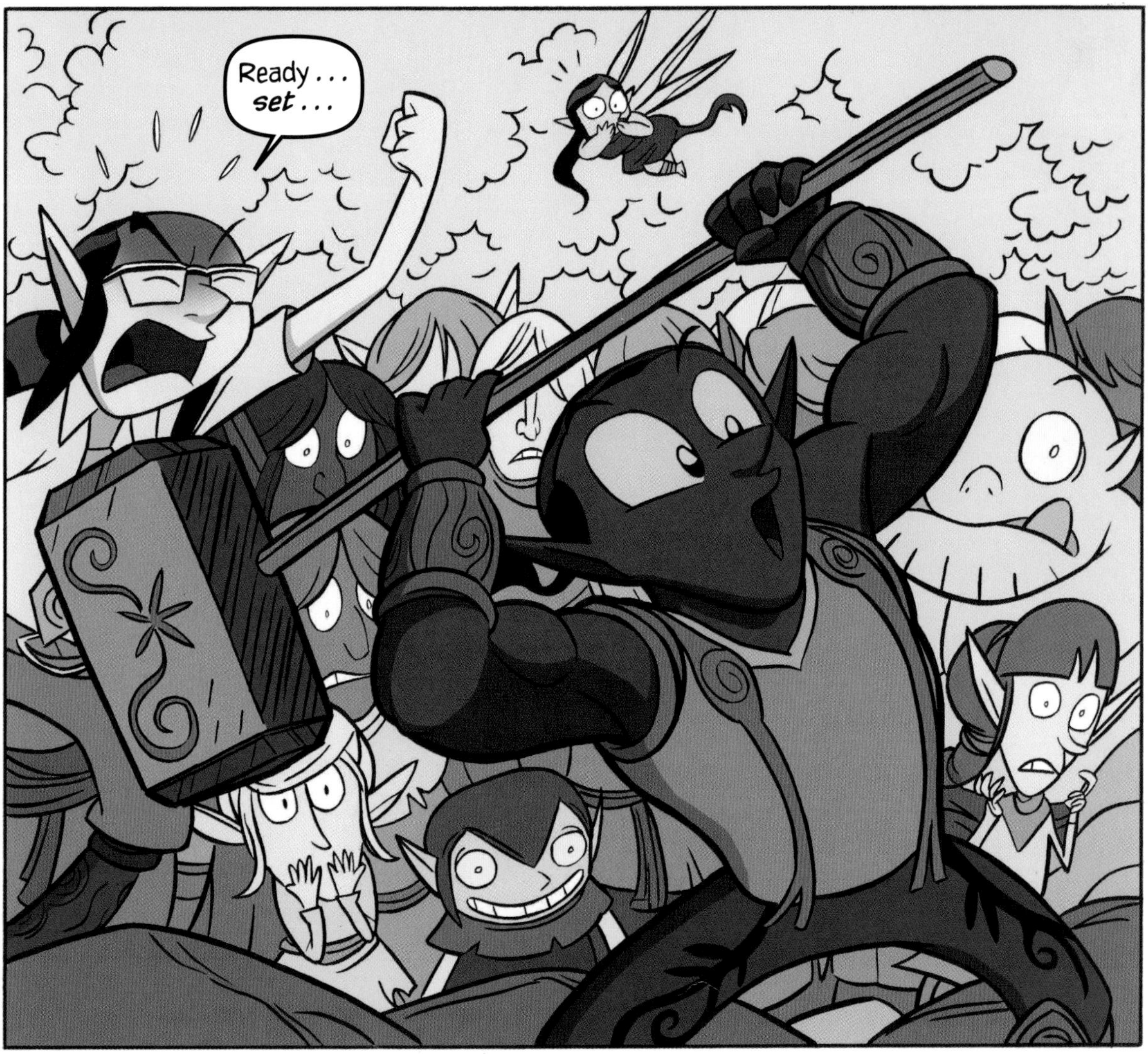
Ready . . . set . . .

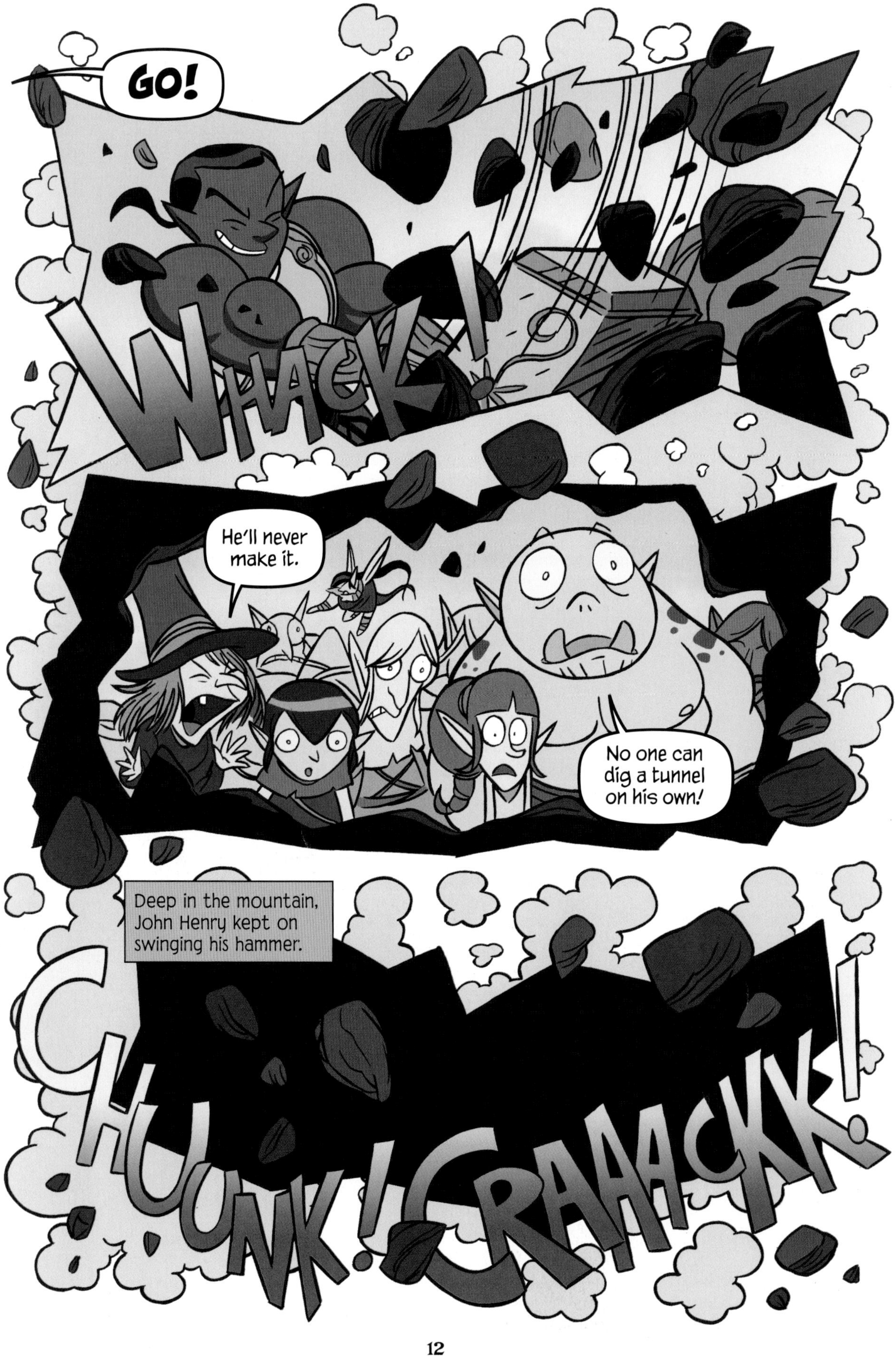
GO!
WHACK!
He'll never make it.
No one can dig a tunnel on his own!
Deep in the mountain, John Henry kept on swinging his hammer.
CHUUNK! CRAAACKK!

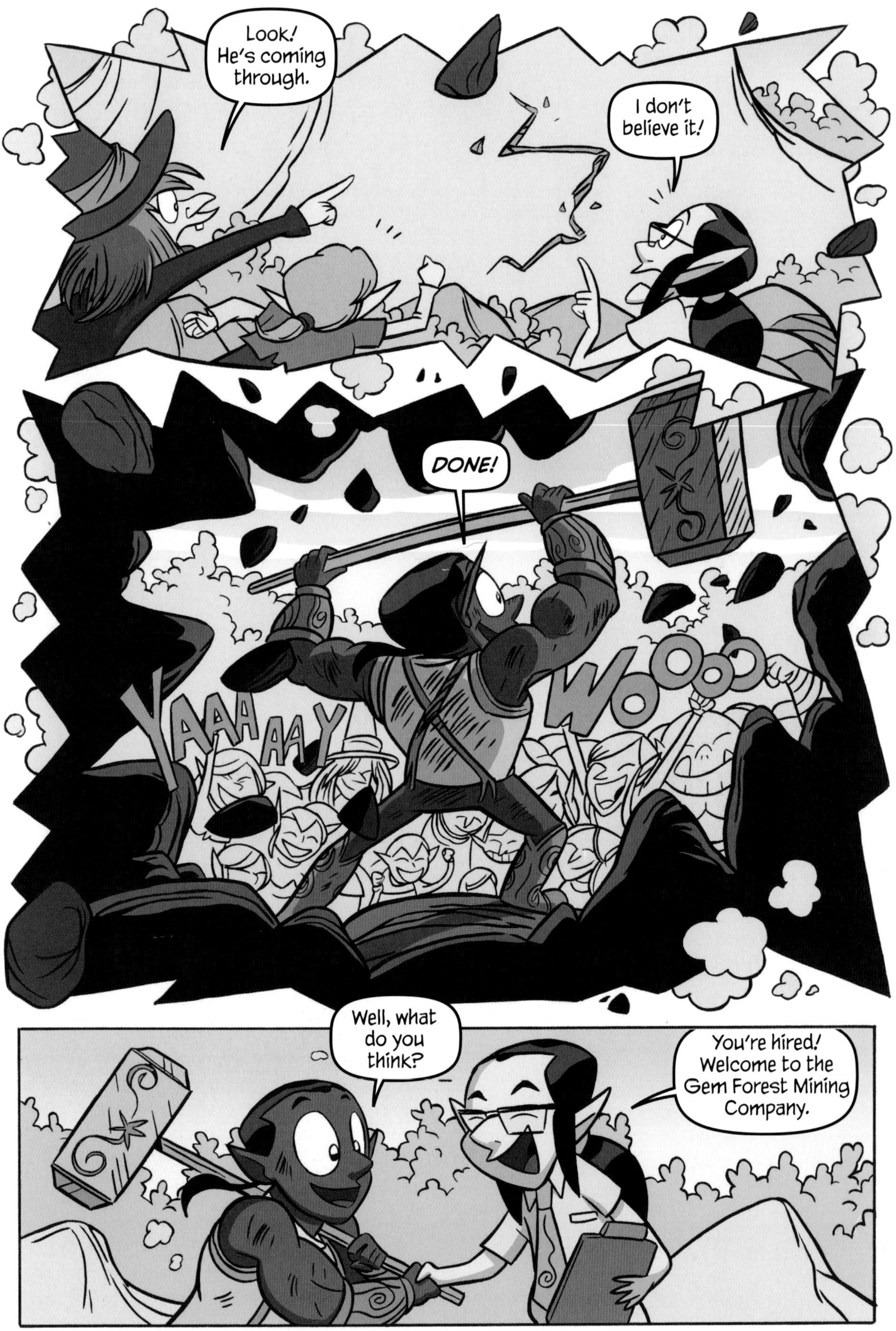

Look! He's coming through.
I don't believe it!
DONE!
YAAAAAY
WOOOOO
Well, what do you think?
You're hired! Welcome to the Gem Forest Mining Company.

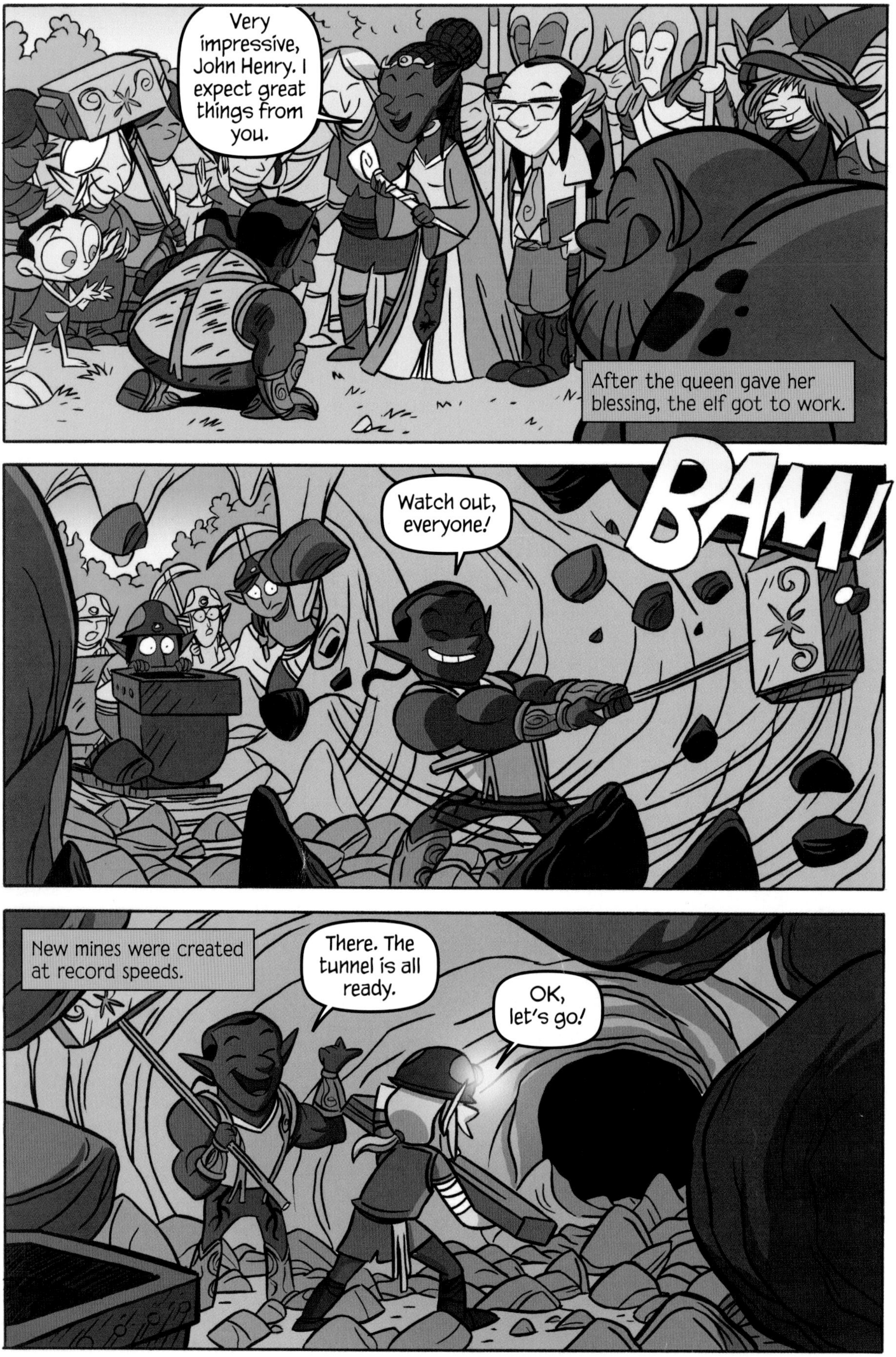
Very impressive, John Henry. I expect great things from you.
After the queen gave her blessing, the elf got to work.
Watch out, everyone!
BAM!
New mines were created at record speeds.
There. The tunnel is all ready.
OK, let's go!

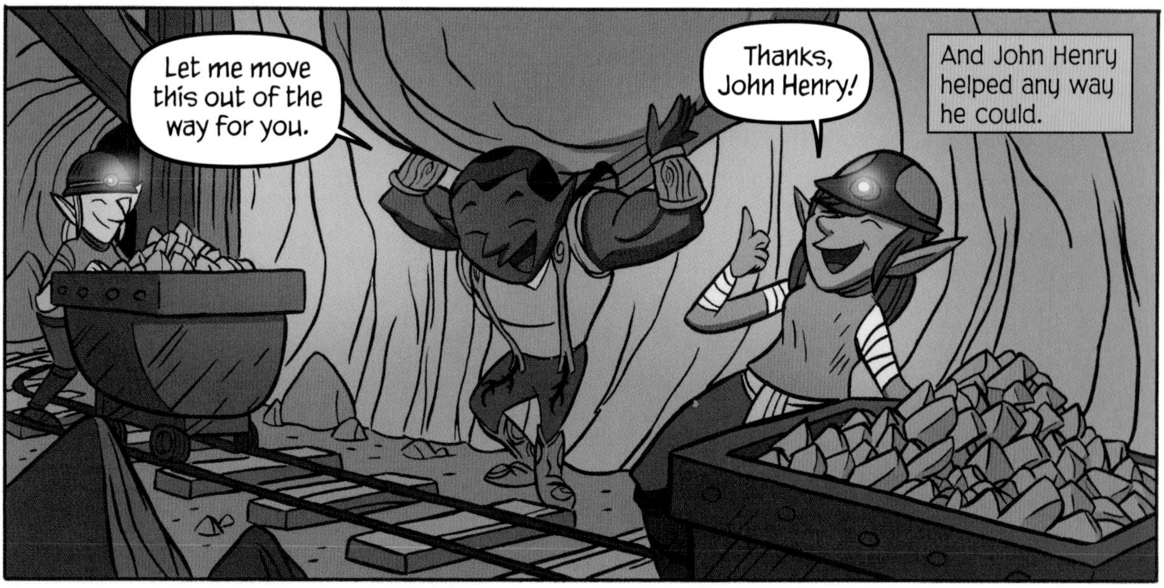
Let me move this out of the way for you.
Thanks, John Henry!
And John Henry helped any way he could.

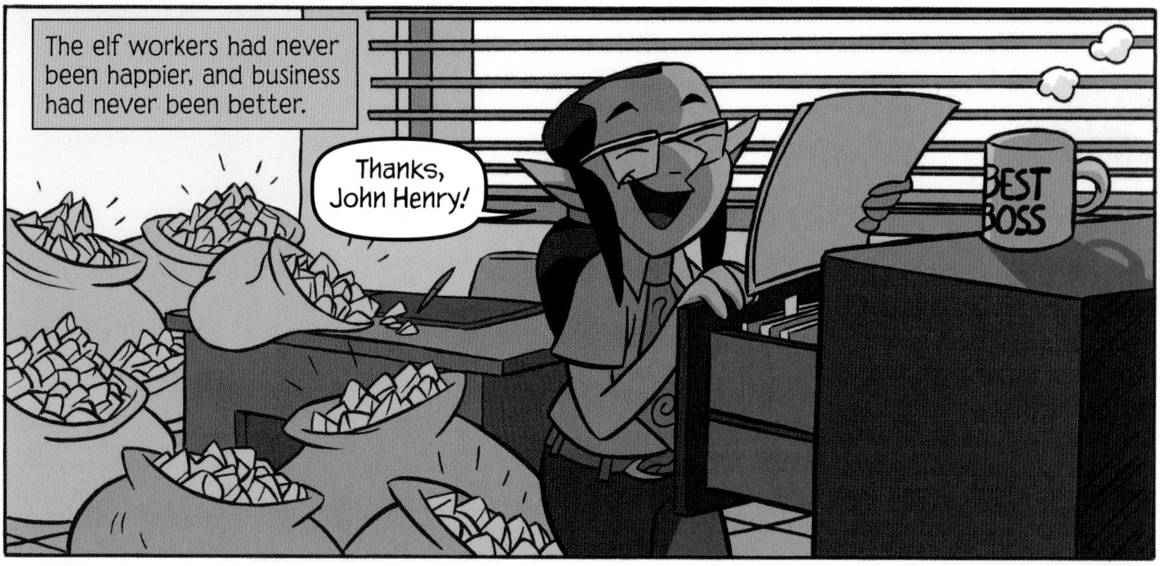
The elf workers had never been happier, and business had never been better.
Thanks, John Henry!
BEST BOSS

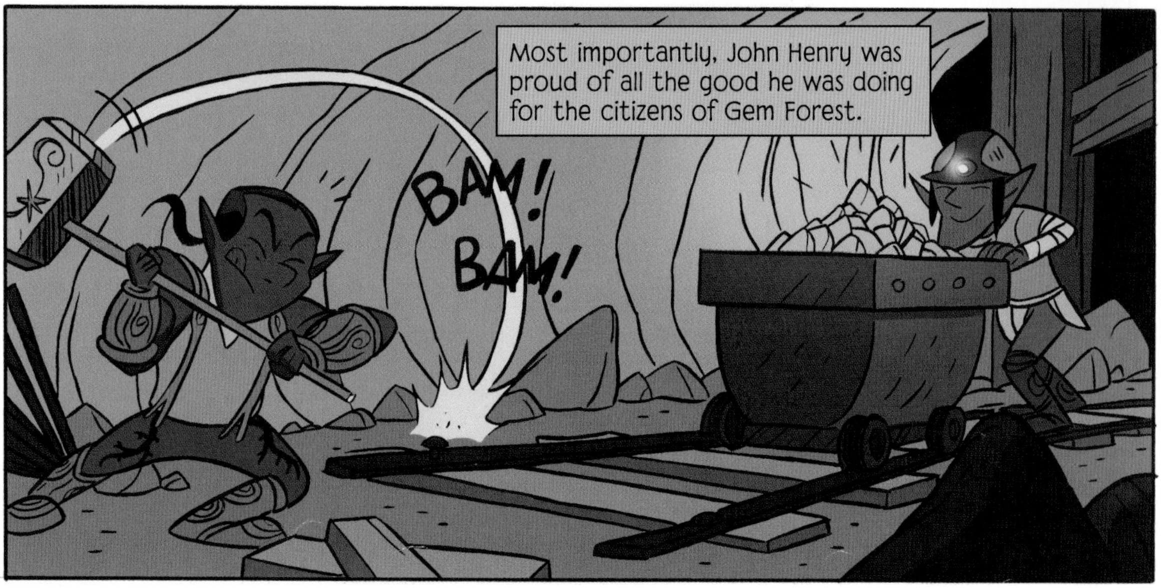
Most importantly, John Henry was proud of all the good he was doing for the citizens of Gem Forest.
BAM! BAM!

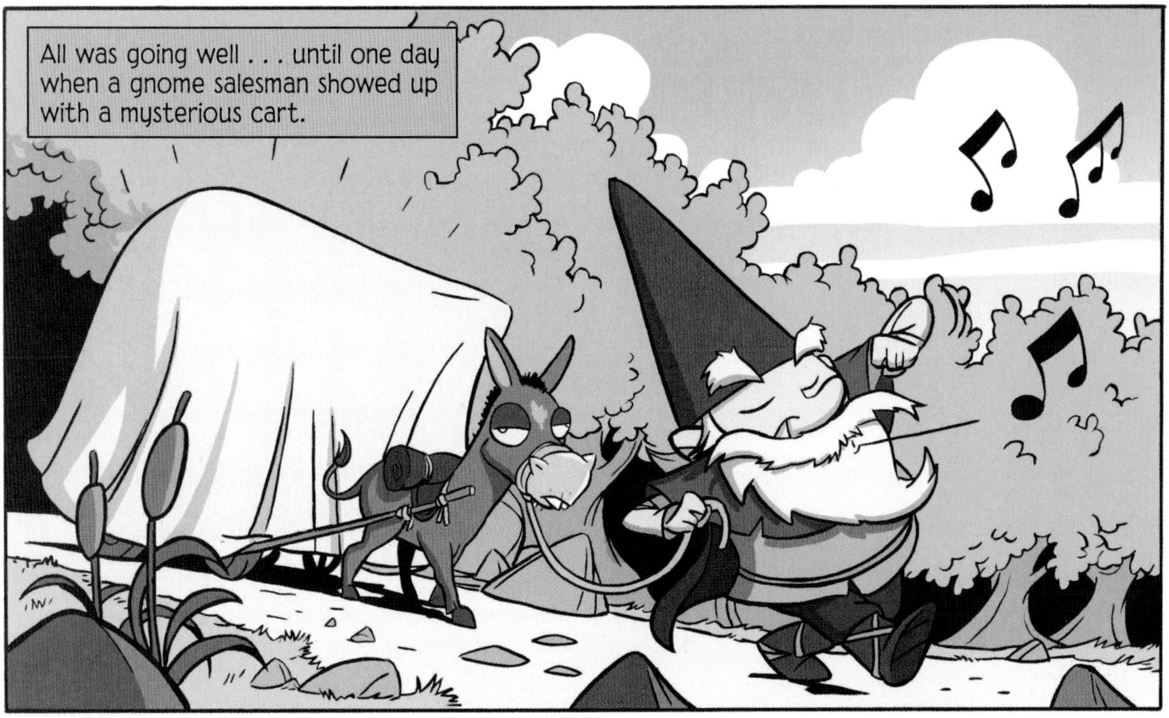
All was going well . . . until one day when a gnome salesman showed up with a mysterious cart.

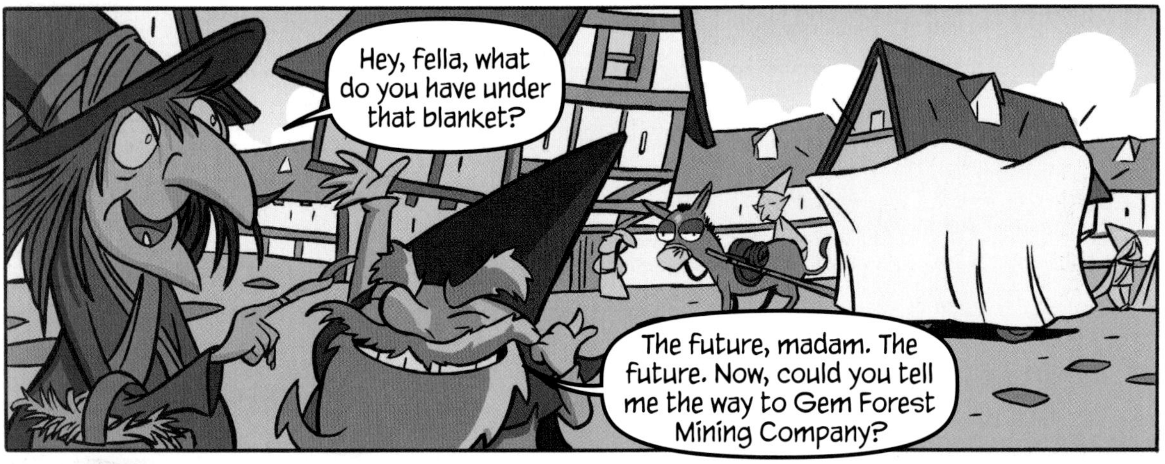
Hey, fella, what do you have under that blanket?
The future, madam. The future. Now, could you tell me the way to Gem Forest Mining Company?

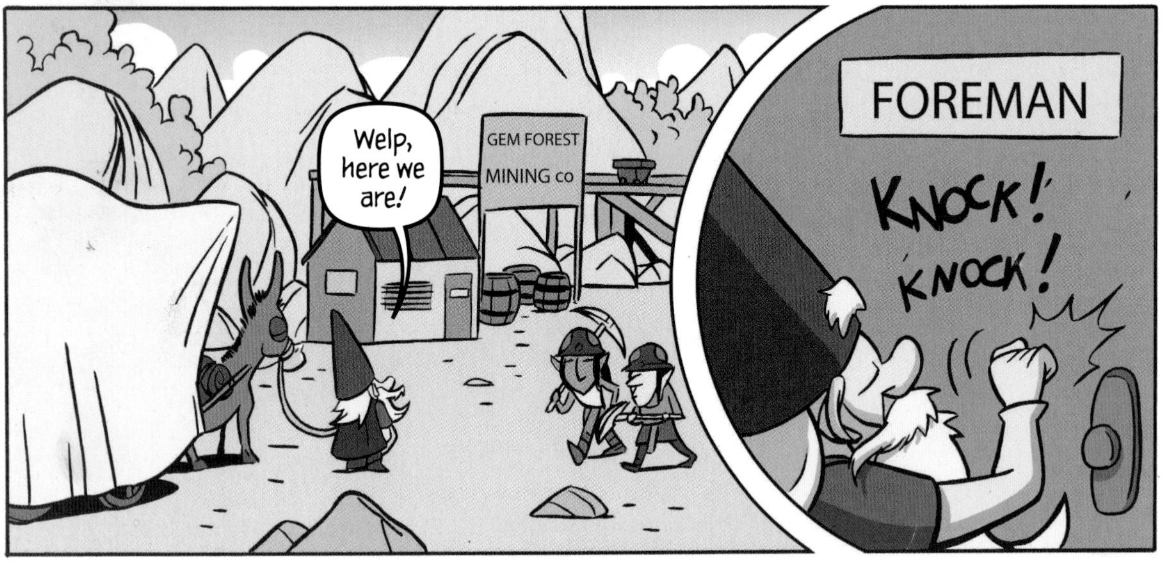
Welp, here we are!
GEM FOREST MINING CO
FOREMAN
KNOCK! KNOCK!

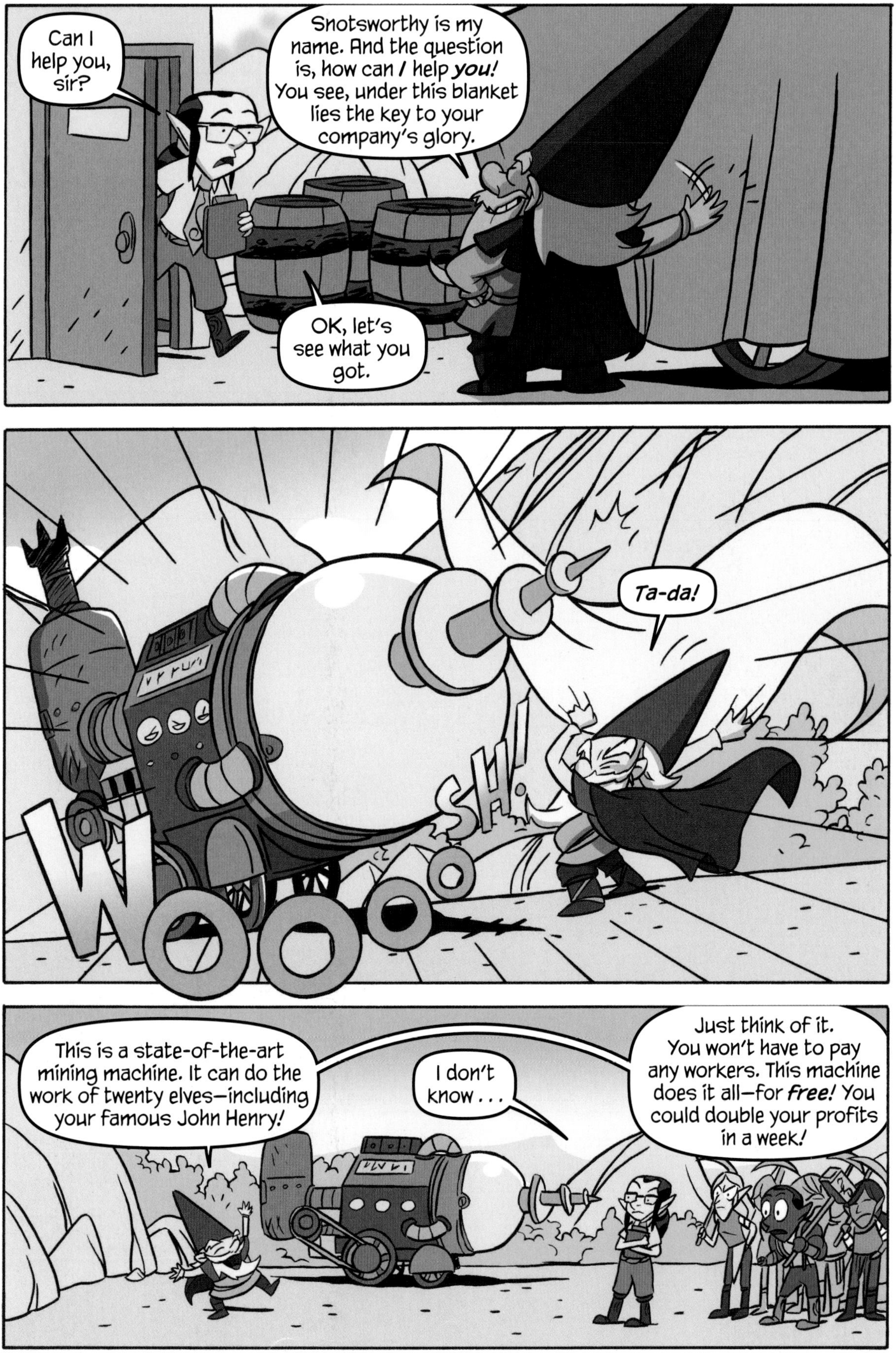
Can I help you, sir?
Snotsworthy is my name. And the question is, how can *I* help ***you!*** You see, under this blanket lies the key to your company's glory.
OK, let's see what you got.
Ta-da!
WOOOOSH!
This is a state-of-the-art mining machine. It can do the work of twenty elves—including your famous John Henry!
I don't know . . .
Just think of it. You won't have to pay any workers. This machine does it all—for ***free!*** You could double your profits in a week!

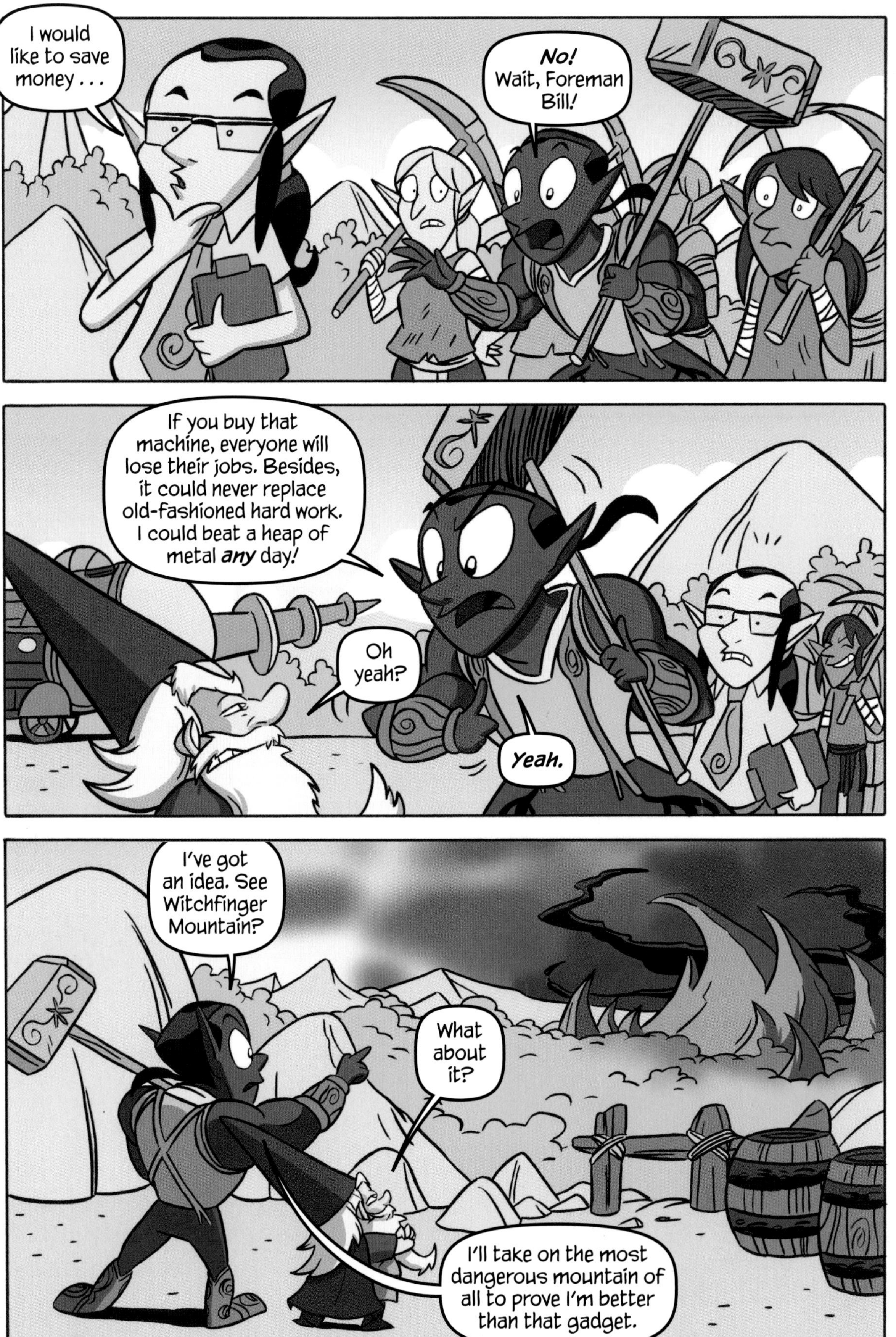
I would like to save money . . .
No! Wait, Foreman Bill!
If you buy that machine, everyone will lose their jobs. Besides, it could never replace old-fashioned hard work. I could beat a heap of metal *any* day!
Oh yeah?
Yeah.
I've got an idea. See Witchfinger Mountain?
What about it?
I'll take on the most dangerous mountain of all to prove I'm better than that gadget.

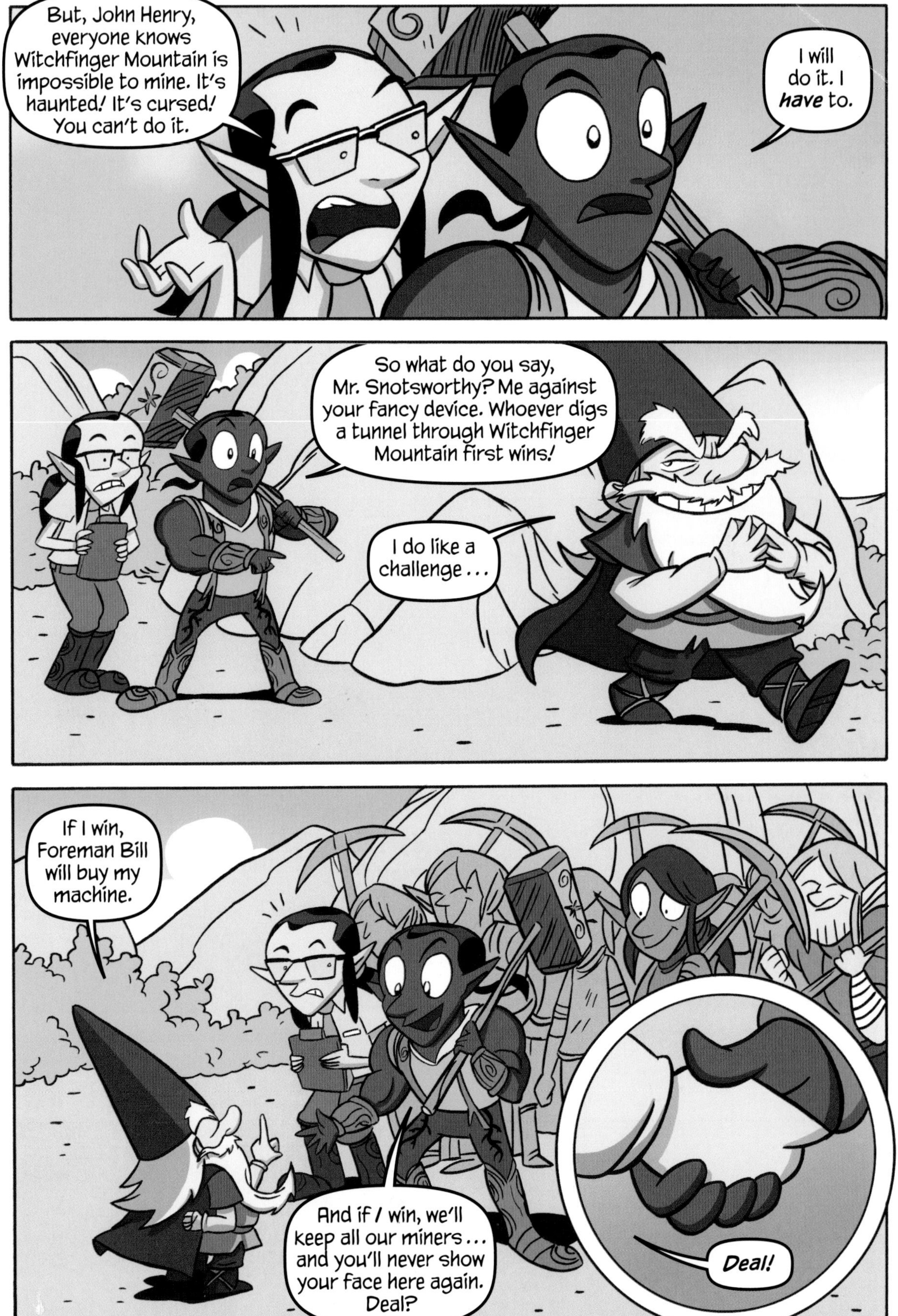
But, John Henry, everyone knows Witchfinger Mountain is impossible to mine. It's haunted! It's cursed! You can't do it.
I will do it. I *have* to.
So what do you say, Mr. Snotsworthy? Me against your fancy device. Whoever digs a tunnel through Witchfinger Mountain first wins!
I do like a challenge . . .
If I win, Foreman Bill will buy my machine.
And if *I* win, we'll keep all our miners . . . and you'll never show your face here again. Deal?
Deal!

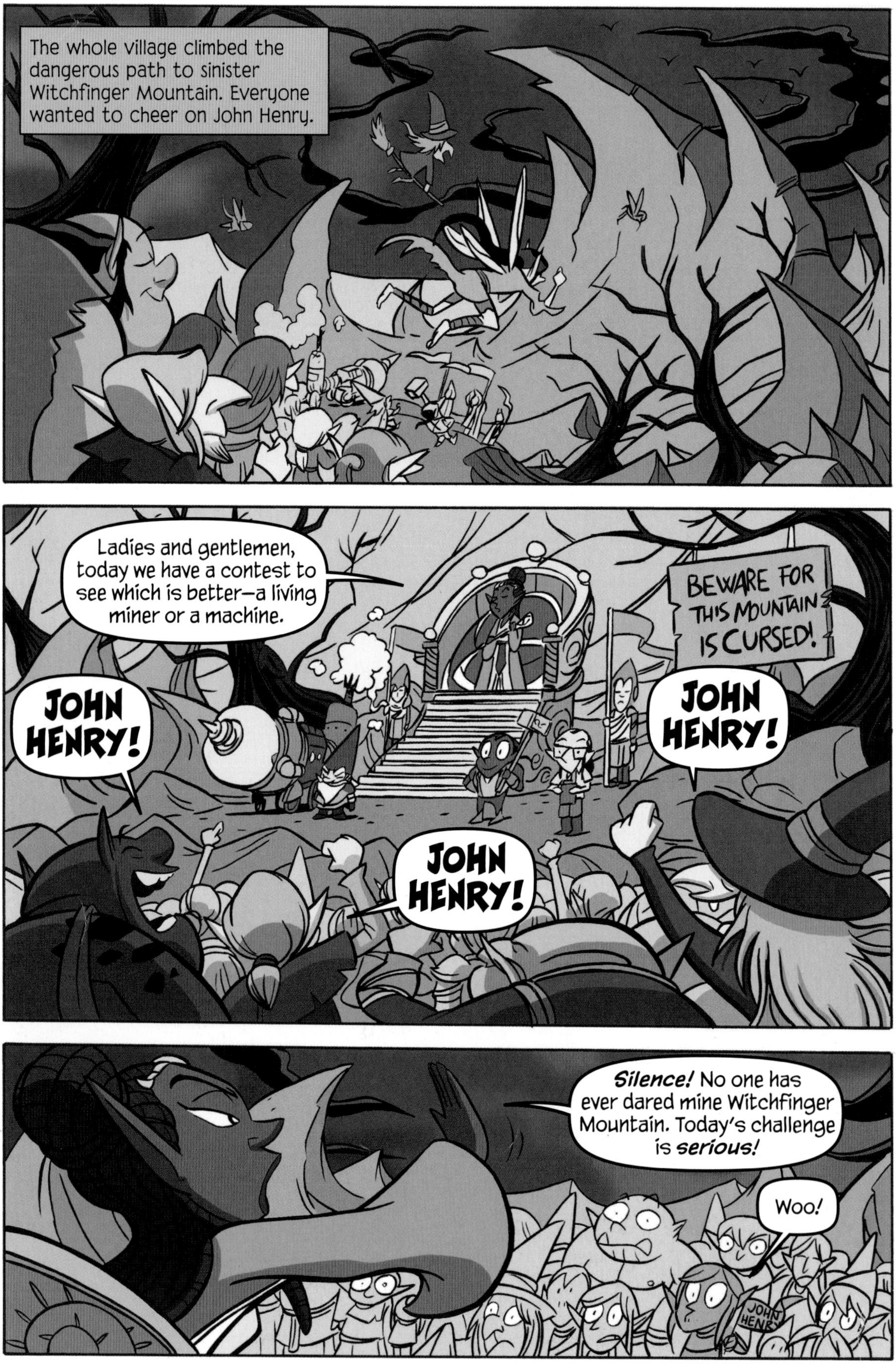
The whole village climbed the dangerous path to sinister Witchfinger Mountain. Everyone wanted to cheer on John Henry.
Ladies and gentlemen, today we have a contest to see which is better—a living miner or a machine.
BEWARE FOR THIS MOUNTAIN IS CURSED!
JOHN HENRY!
JOHN HENRY!
JOHN HENRY!
Silence! No one has ever dared mine Witchfinger Mountain. Today's challenge is *serious!*
Woo!

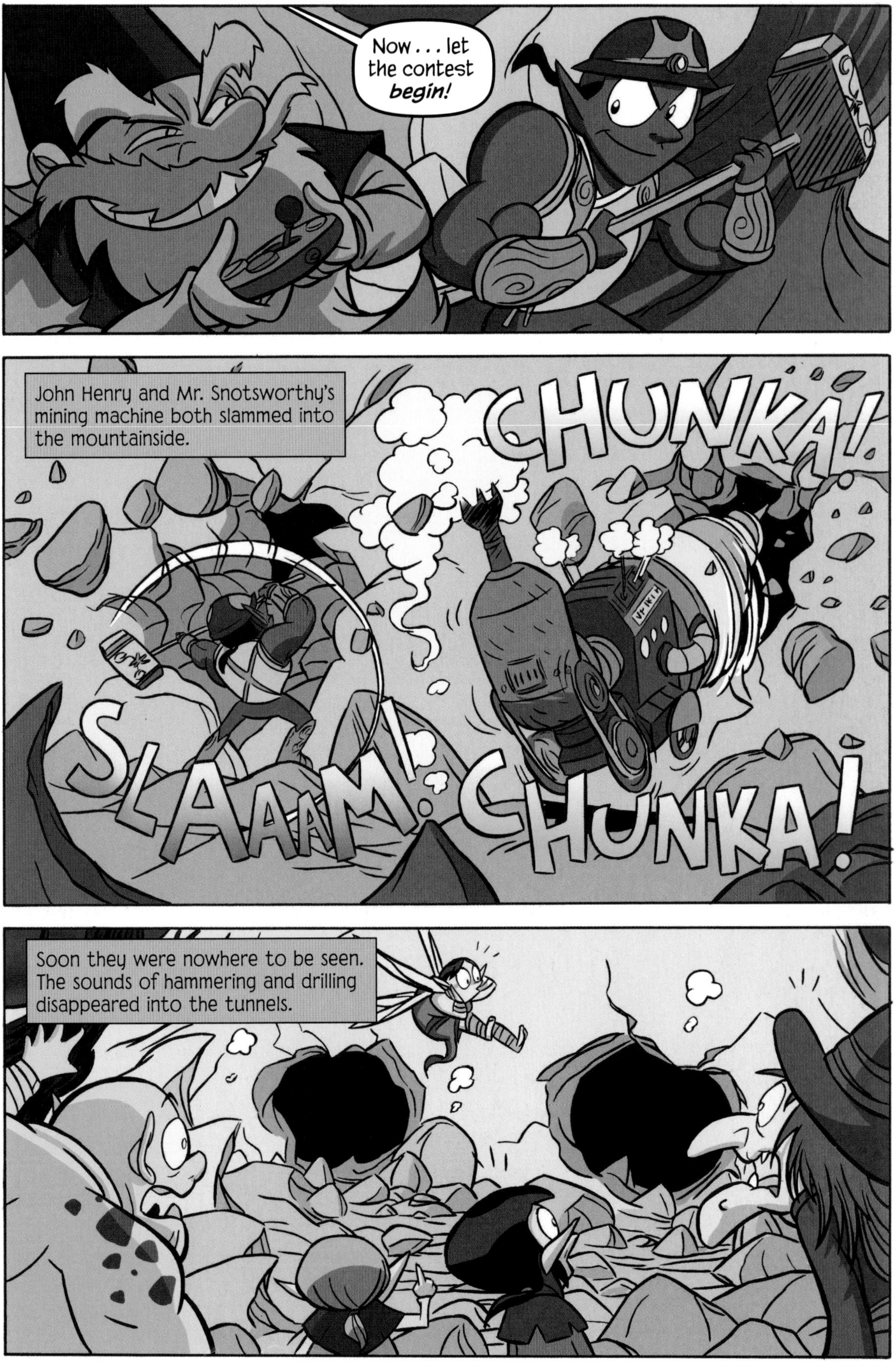

Now . . . let the contest *begin!*
John Henry and Mr. Snotsworthy's mining machine both slammed into the mountainside.
CHUNKA!
SLAAAM!
CHUNKA!
Soon they were nowhere to be seen. The sounds of hammering and drilling disappeared into the tunnels.

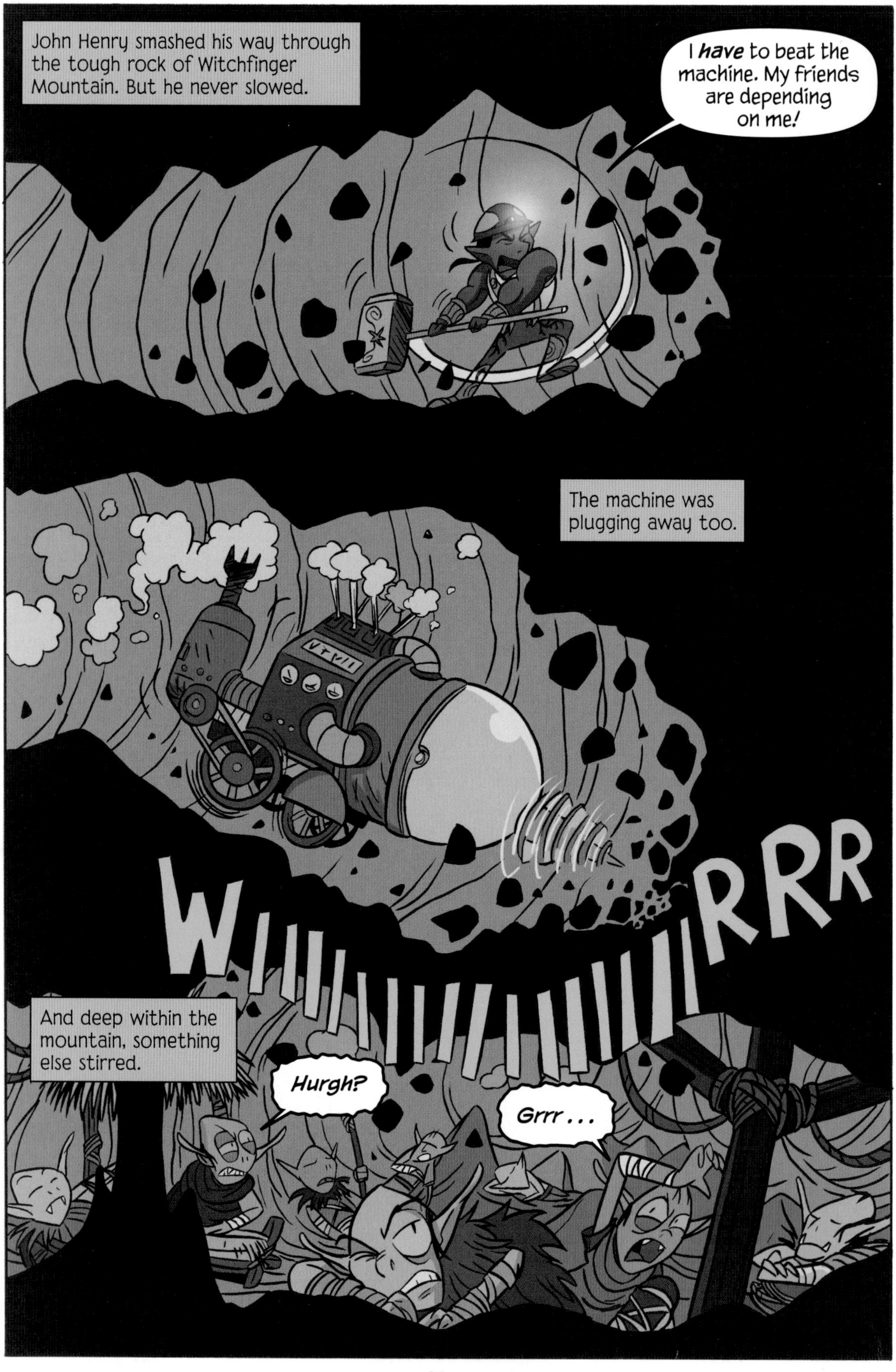

John Henry smashed his way through the tough rock of Witchfinger Mountain. But he never slowed.
I *have* to beat the machine. My friends are depending on me!
The machine was plugging away too.
WIIIIIIIIIIIIIIIIIRRR
And deep within the mountain, something else stirred.
Hurgh?
Grrr . . .

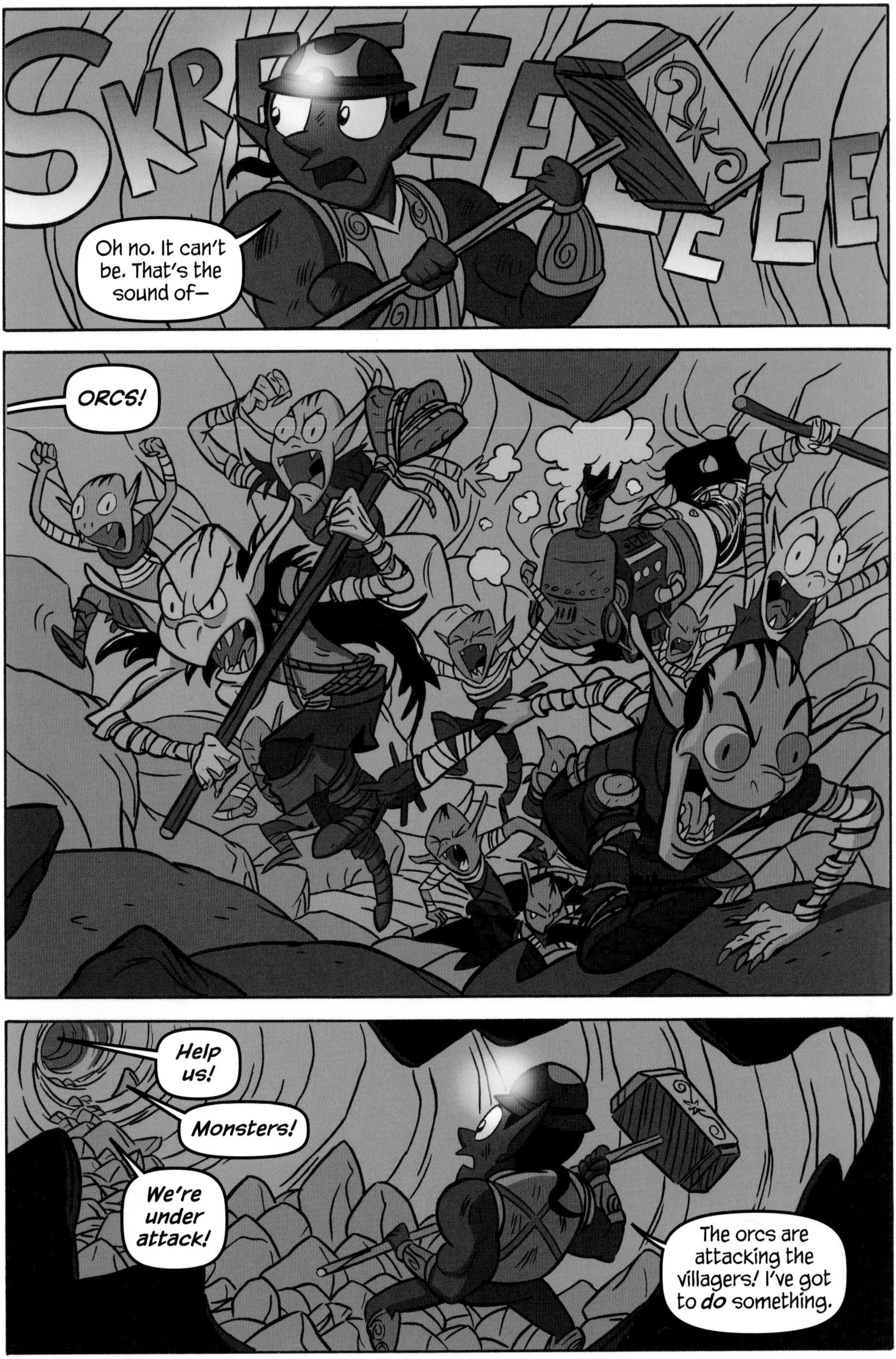
SKREEEEEEEEEE
Oh no. It can't be. That's the sound of—
ORCS!
Help us!
Monsters!
We're under attack!
The orcs are attacking the villagers! I've got to *do* something.

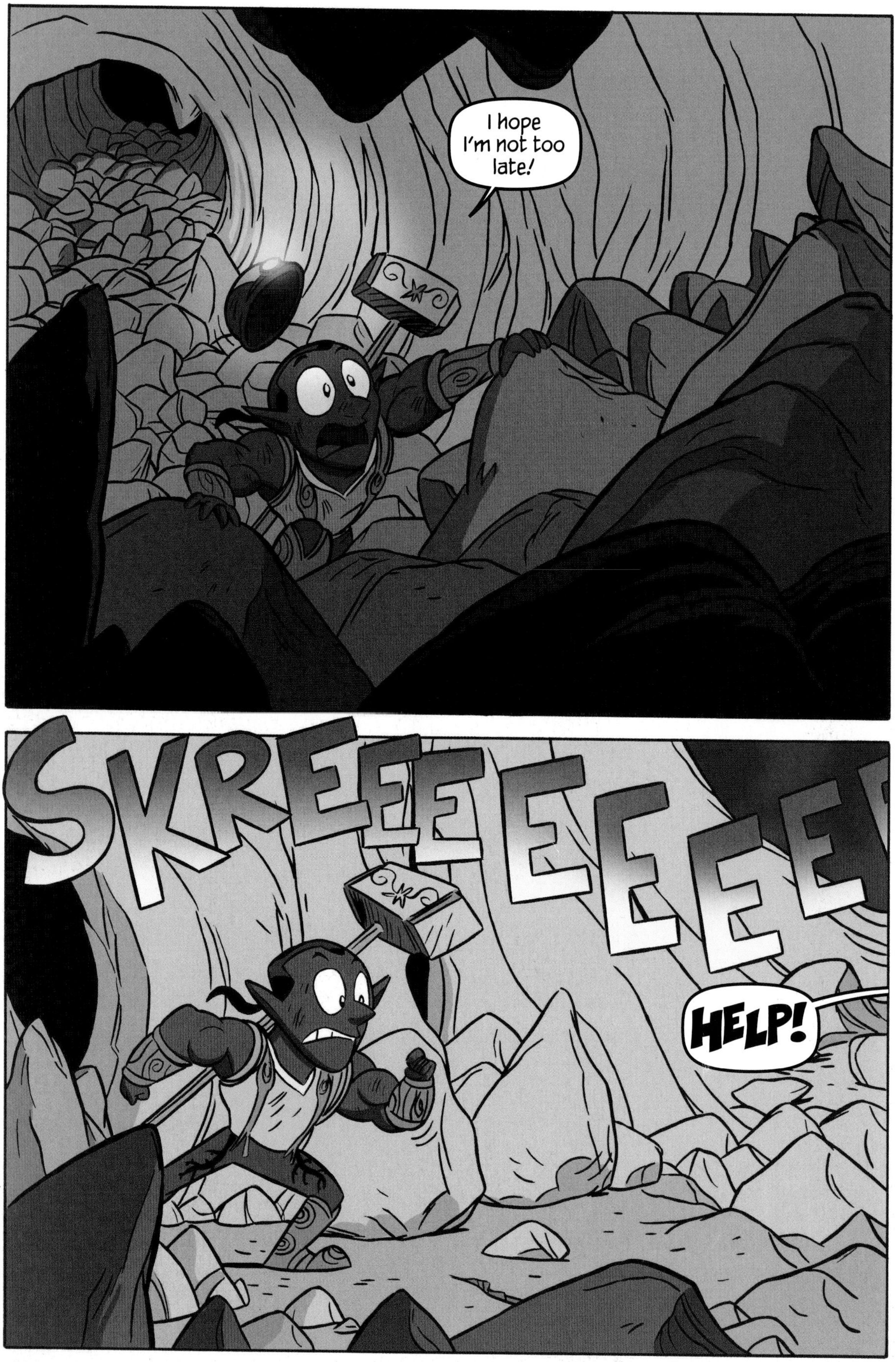
I hope I'm not too late!
SKREEEEEEE
HELP!

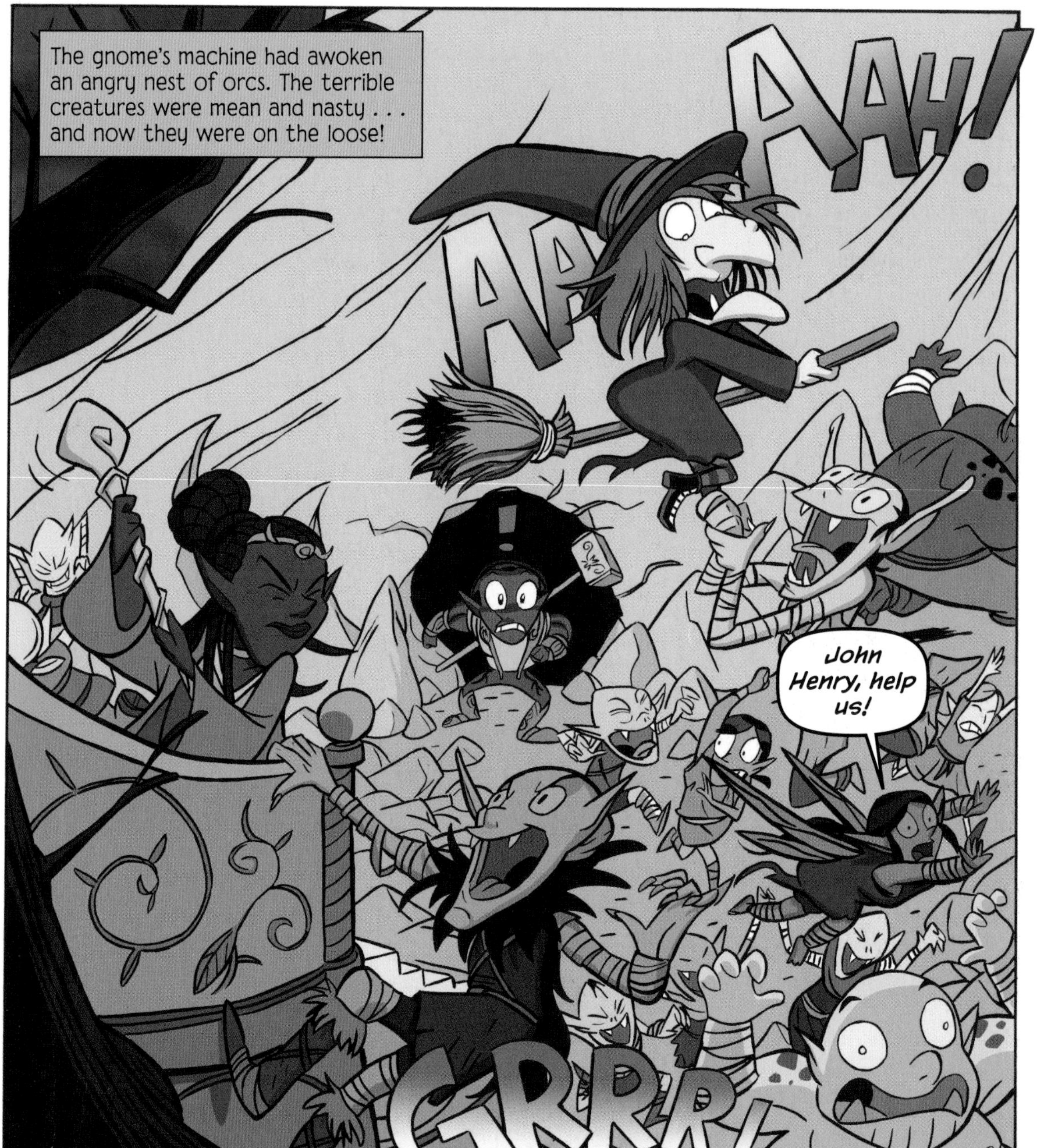
The gnome's machine had awoken an angry nest of orcs. The terrible creatures were mean and nasty . . . and now they were on the loose!
AAAAH!
John Henry, help us!
GRRR!

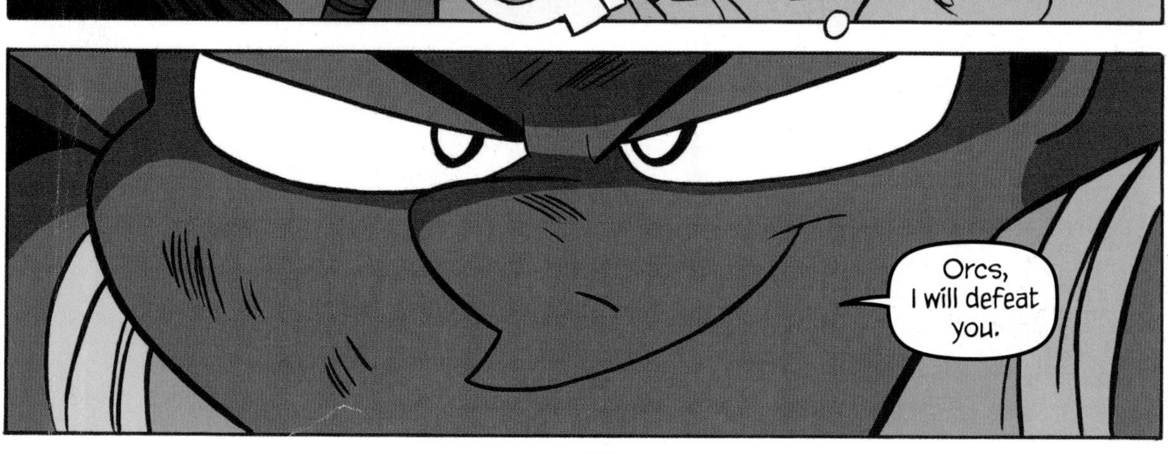
Orcs, I will defeat you.

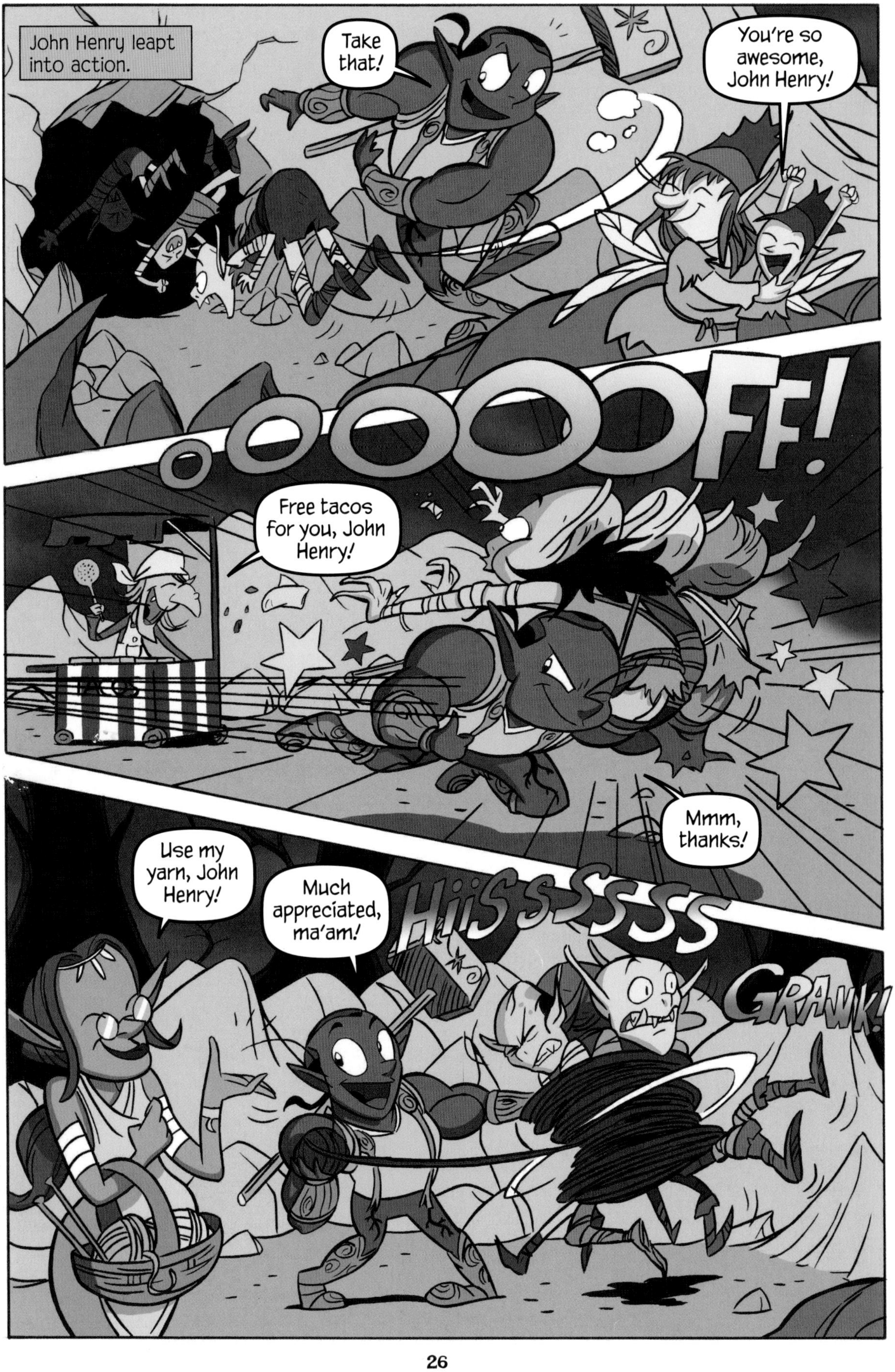
John Henry leapt into action.
Take that!
You're so awesome, John Henry!
OOOOOFF!
Free tacos for you, John Henry!
TACOS
Mmm, thanks!
Use my yarn, John Henry!
Much appreciated, ma'am!
HiiSSSSSS
GRANK!

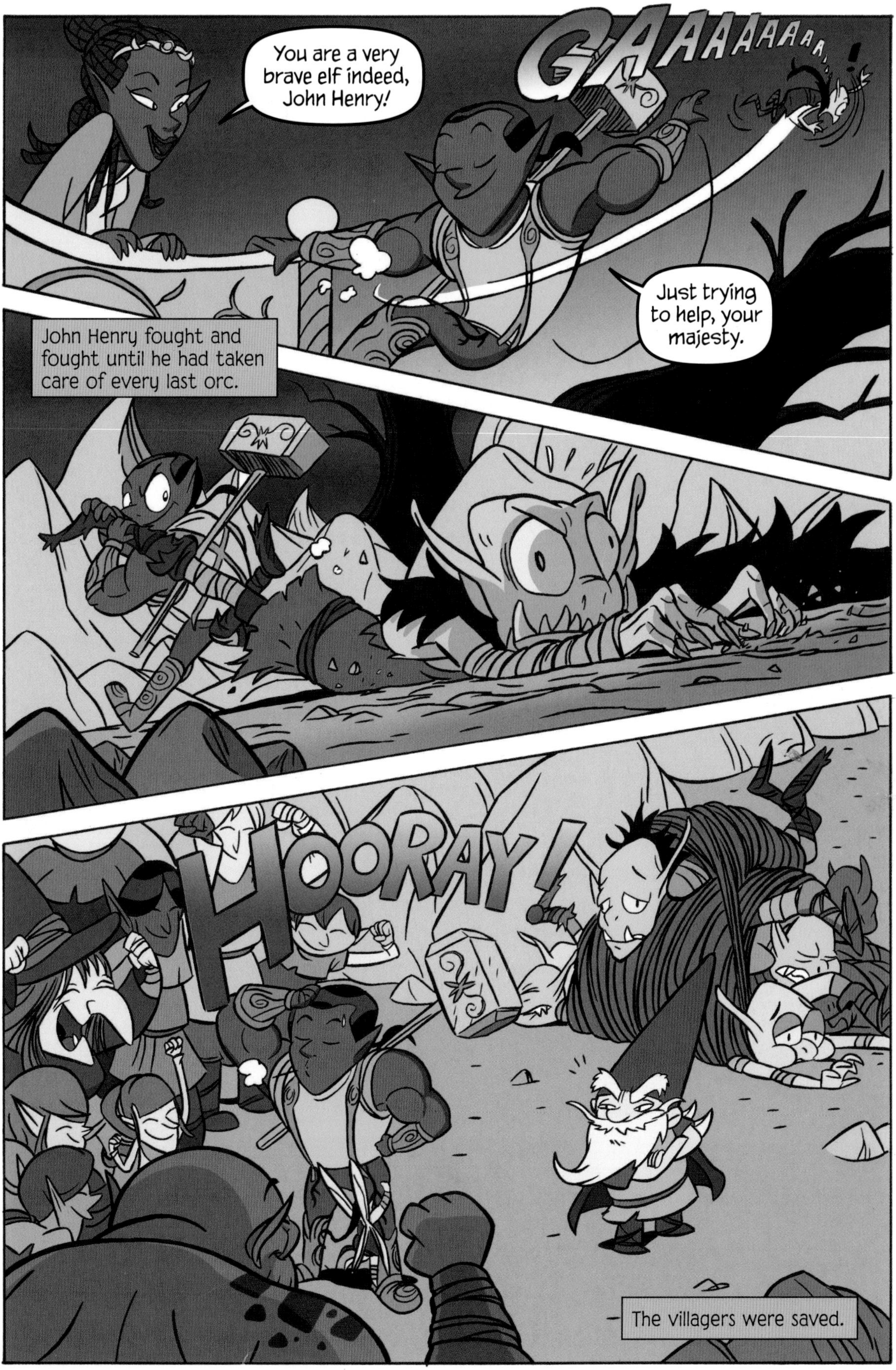
GAAAAAAAA!
You are a very brave elf indeed, John Henry!
Just trying to help, your majesty.
John Henry fought and fought until he had taken care of every last orc.
HOORAY!
The villagers were saved.

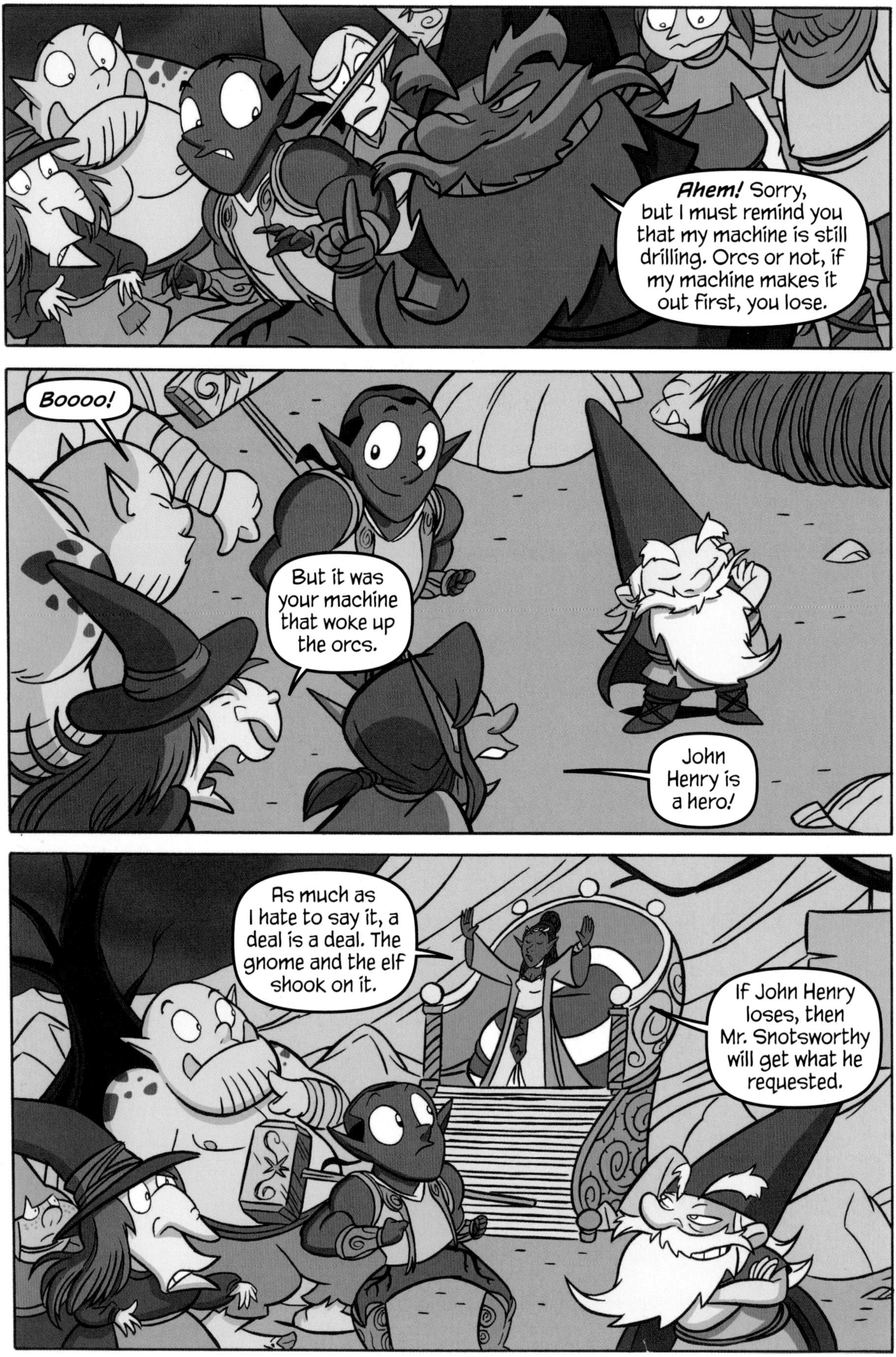
Ahem! Sorry, but I must remind you that my machine is still drilling. Orcs or not, if my machine makes it out first, you lose.
Boooo!
But it was your machine that woke up the orcs.
John Henry is a hero!
As much as I hate to say it, a deal is a deal. The gnome and the elf shook on it.
If John Henry loses, then Mr. Snotsworthy will get what he requested.

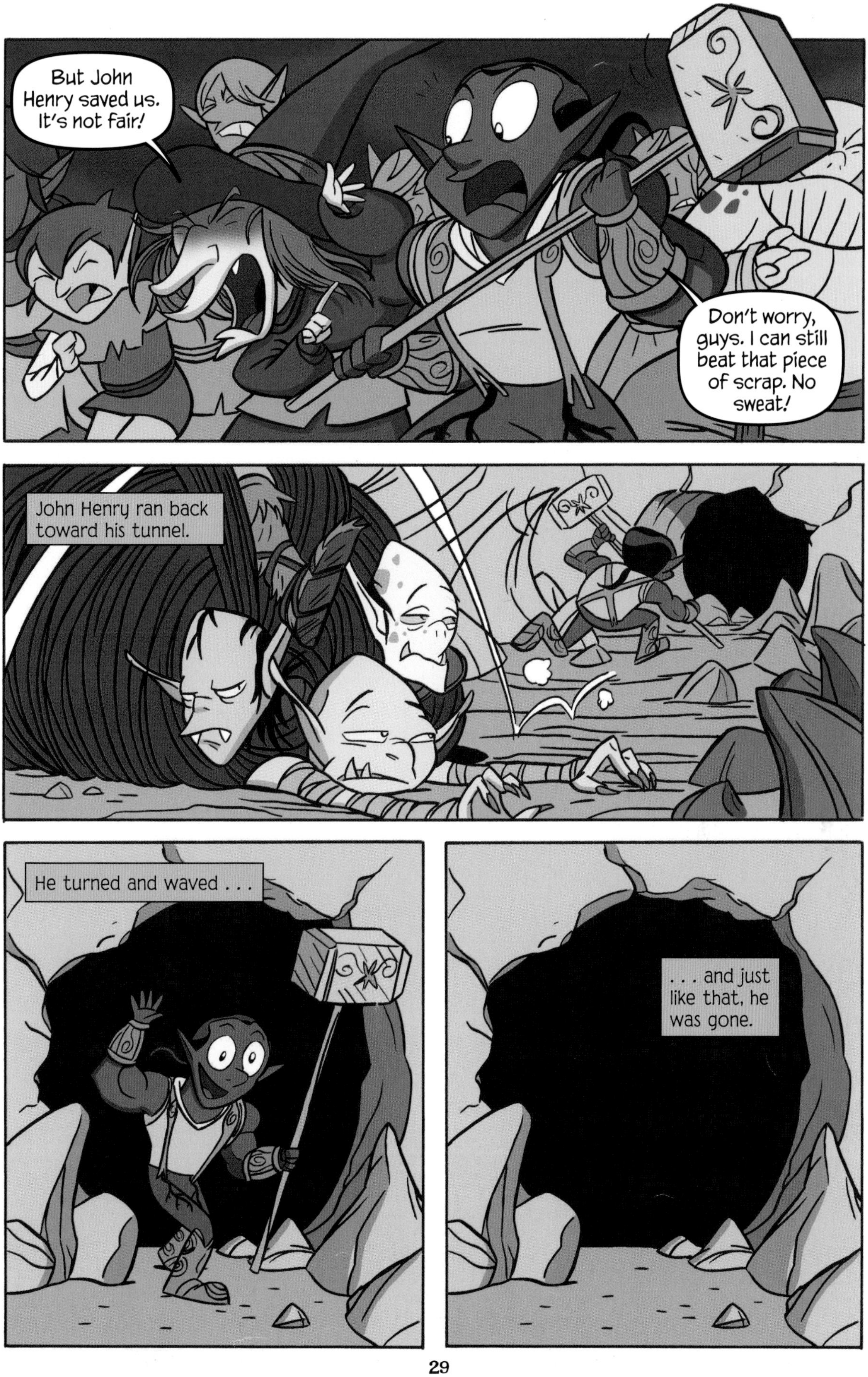
But John Henry saved us. It's not fair!
Don't worry, guys. I can still beat that piece of scrap. No sweat!
John Henry ran back toward his tunnel.
He turned and waved . . .
. . . and just like that, he was gone.

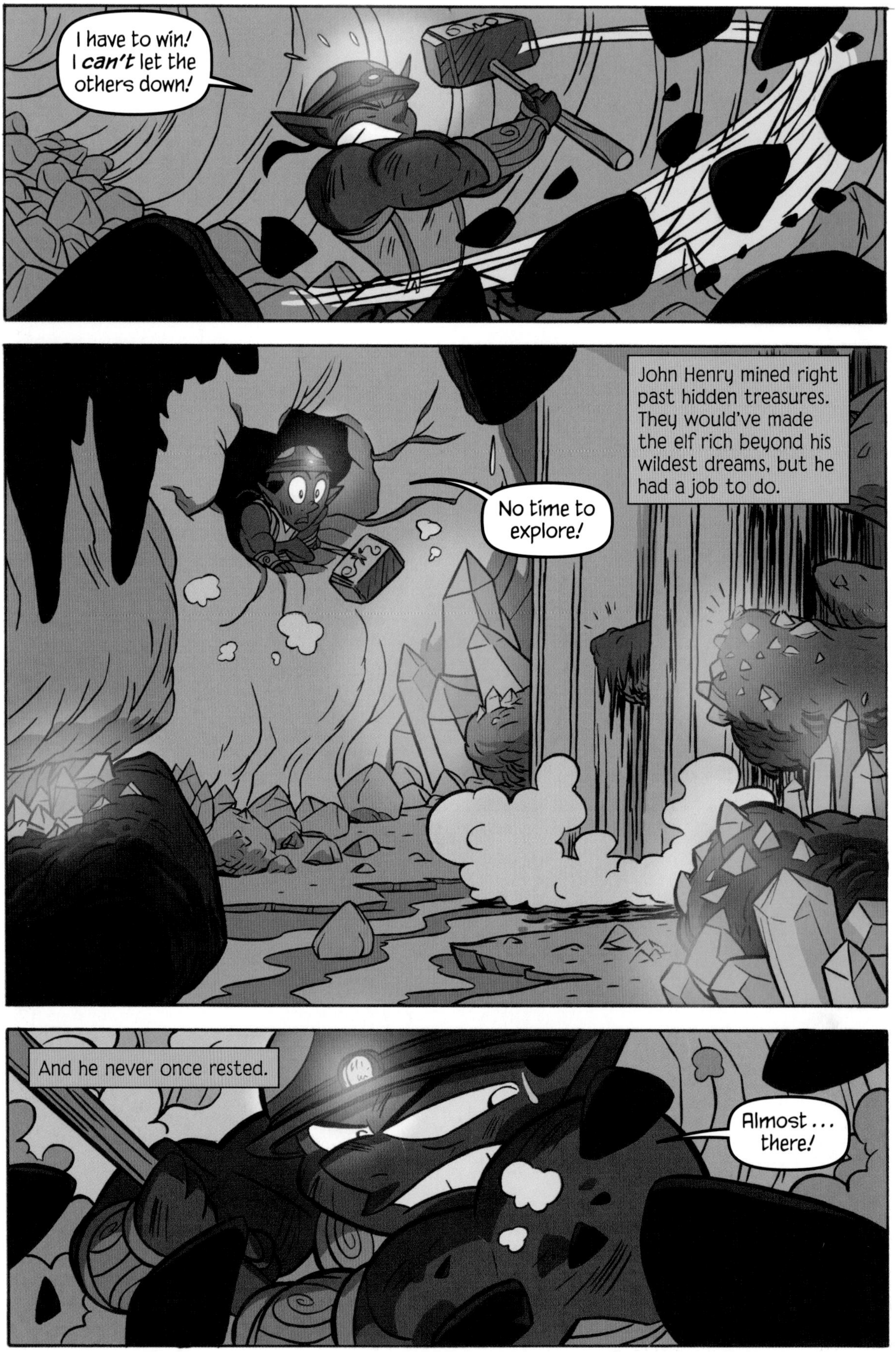
I have to win! I ***can't*** let the others down!
John Henry mined right past hidden treasures. They would've made the elf rich beyond his wildest dreams, but he had a job to do.
No time to explore!
And he never once rested.
Almost . . . there!

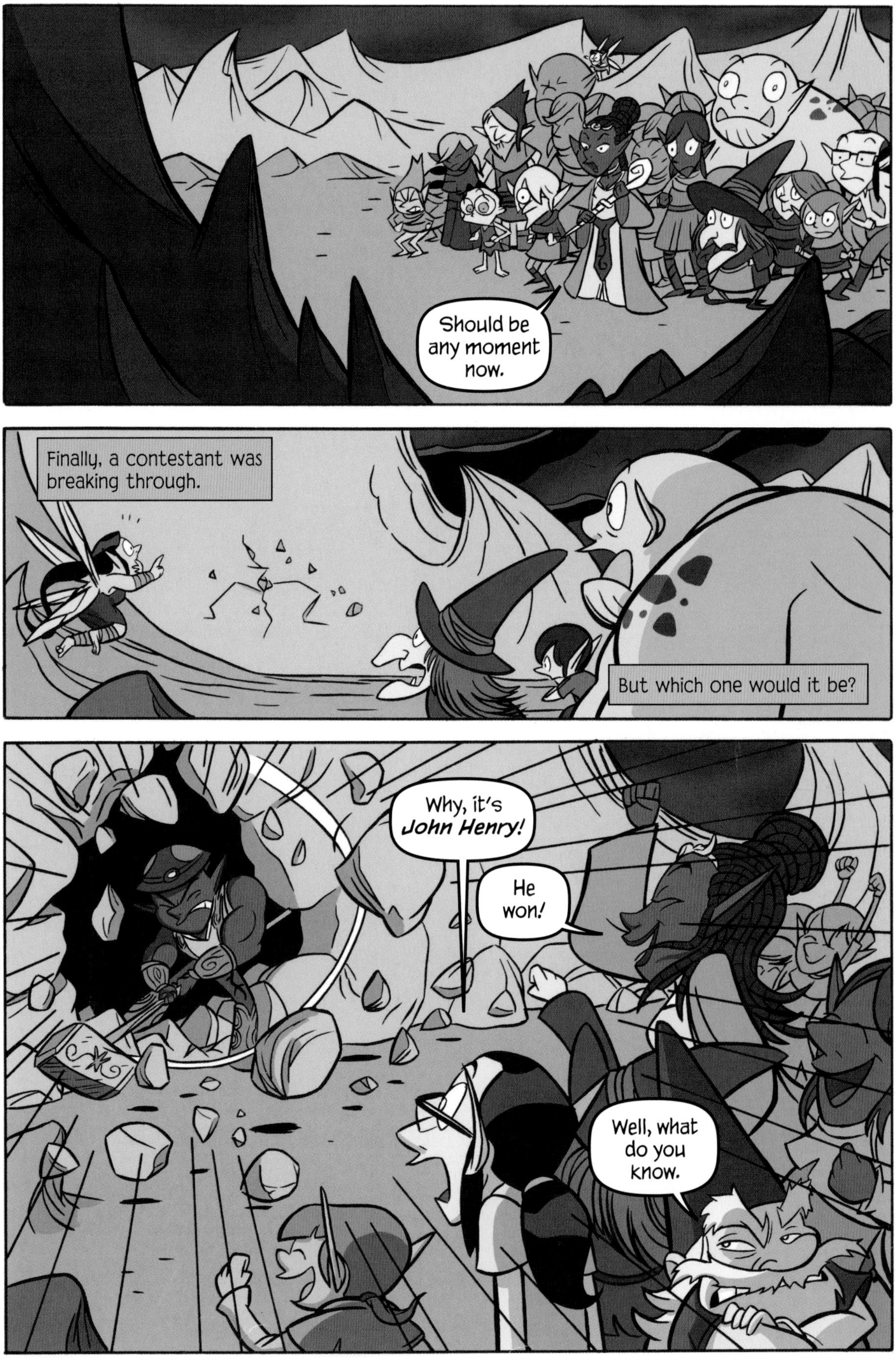
Should be any moment now.
Finally, a contestant was breaking through.
But which one would it be?
Why, it's *John Henry!*
He won!
Well, what do you know.

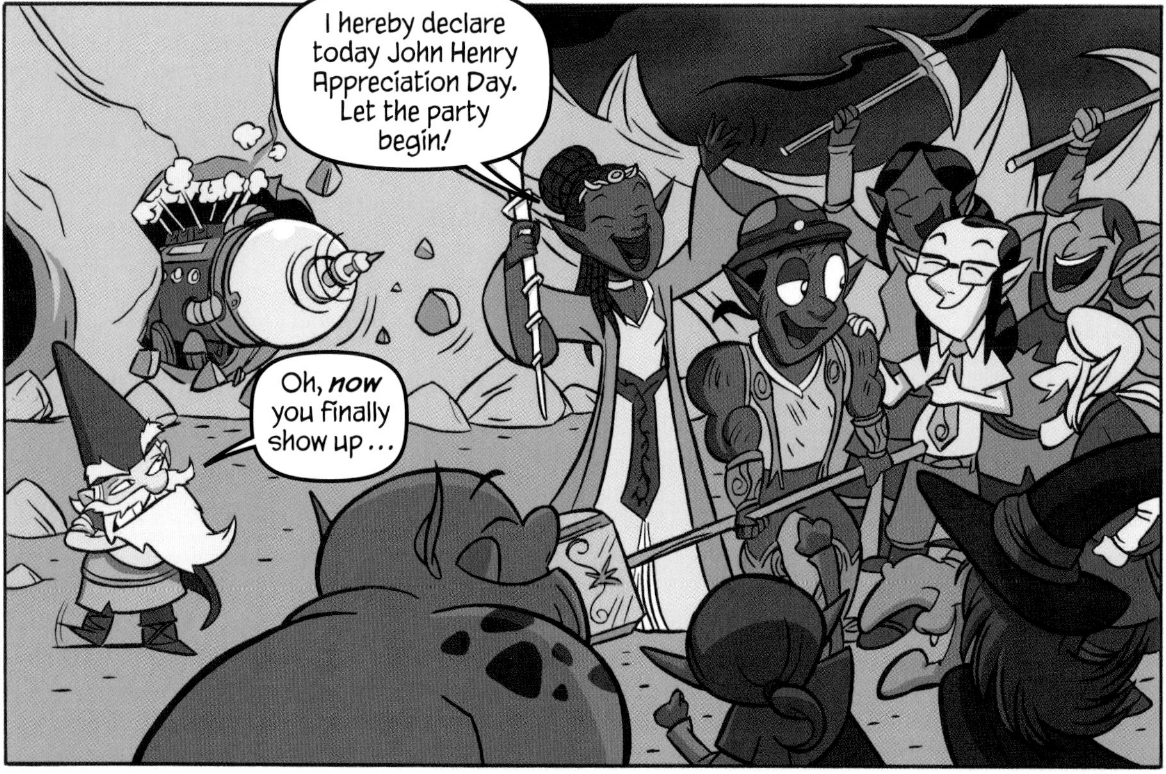
I hereby declare today John Henry Appreciation Day. Let the party begin!
Oh, *now* you finally show up . . .

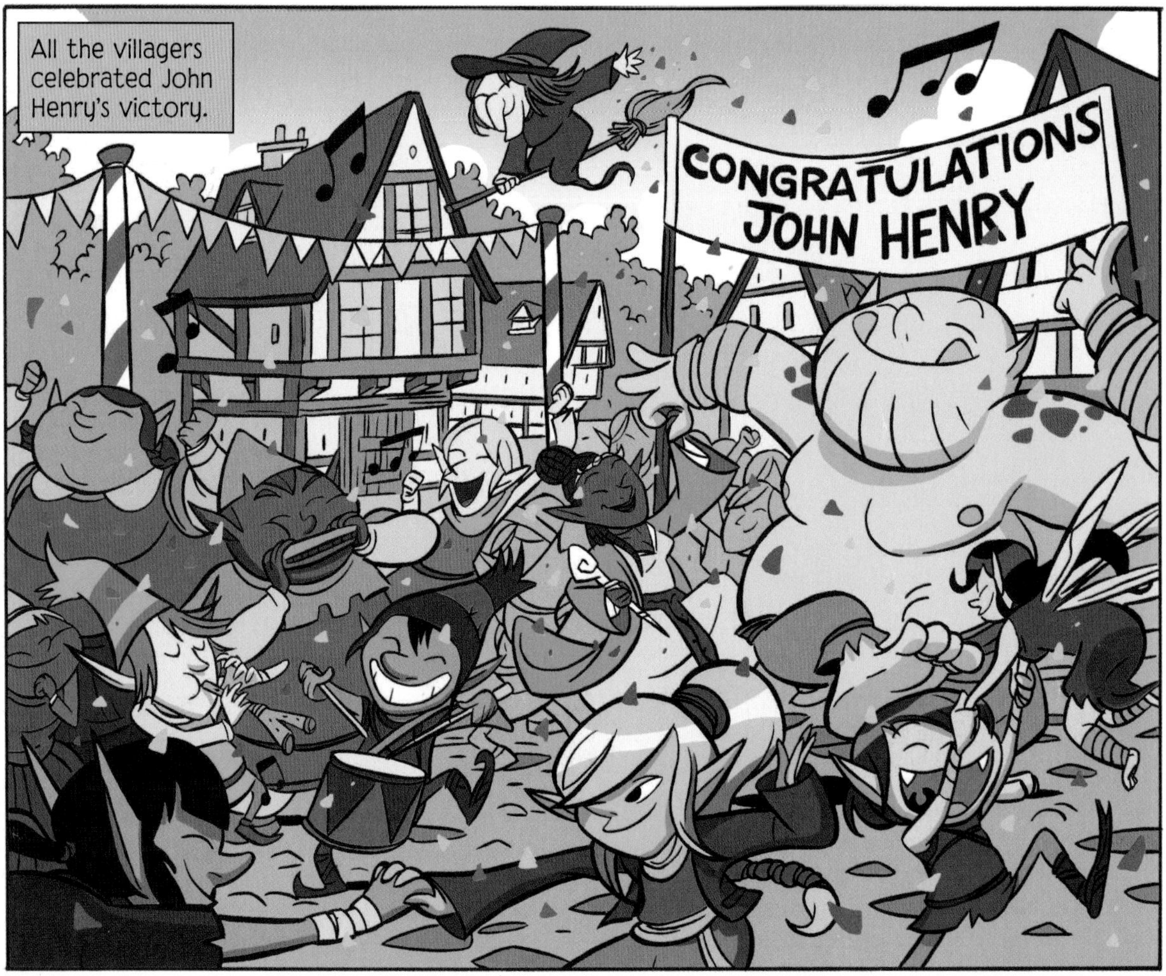
All the villagers celebrated John Henry's victory.
CONGRATULATIONS JOHN HENRY

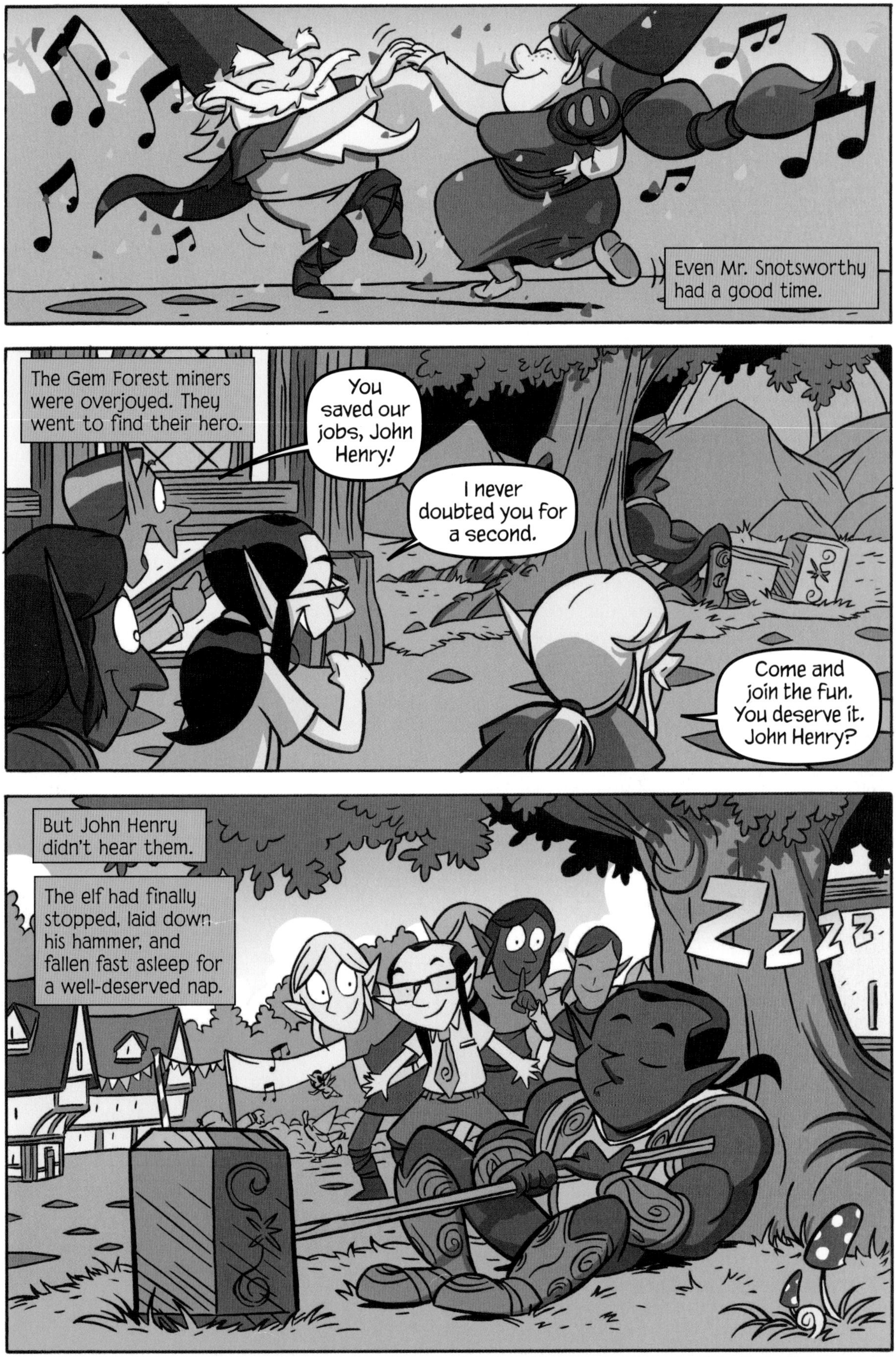
Even Mr. Snotsworthy had a good time.
The Gem Forest miners were overjoyed. They went to find their hero.
You saved our jobs, John Henry!
I never doubted you for a second.
Come and join the fun. You deserve it. John Henry?
But John Henry didn't hear them.
The elf had finally stopped, laid down his hammer, and fallen fast asleep for a well-deserved nap.
ZZZZ

ALL ABOUT THE ORIGINAL TALE!

A folktale is a story that's told over and over again and passed down through generations. Tales of an incredible steel-driver named John Henry were popular among railroad workers in the 1870s. They sang songs about the hammering man. The stories may have been based on a real person, but the legend of John Henry spread until he became a true American folk hero.

Some tales say when John Henry was born, thunder shook the earth. People claim the mighty babe came out with a hammer in his hand. But the real John Henry was born into slavery and had to work long and hard each day. After the Civil War, he was free but life was still difficult. He took a dangerous job as a steel-driver on the railroad. With a hammer, he hit steel spikes into rock to clear it out of the way of the rails. It was said John Henry could do more work in one day than others could do in a week.

Soon the tracks came to Big Bend Mountain. It was too large to go around, so a tunnel would have to be built through it! A salesman arrived at camp saying he had an amazing steam-powered drill. It could work faster than any man and finish the tunnel in no time. John Henry knew if the bosses bought it, everyone would be put out of work. So he bet he could drill farther than the machine.

The race started. The drill whirred, and John Henry swung his twenty-pound hammer. The mountain shook so much that people thought it was crumbling, but it was just John Henry pounding away. When the contest was over, the machine had drilled seven feet—and John Henry had gone fourteen! The workers cheered. But John Henry had pushed himself so hard that he couldn't go anymore. He laid down and died, with his hammer in his hand.

A FAR OUT GUIDE TO THE TALE'S FANTASY TWISTS

In this story, John Henry isn't an extraordinary man. He's an extraordinary ELF!

United States railroads have been swapped out for fantasy-land gemstone mines.

Instead of only racing a machine, John Henry also battles (and defeats!) terrifying orcs.

There aren't any funerals in this version. John Henry just needs a long nap and he'll be back at full strength!

VISUAL QUESTIONS

1

In the original folktale, John Henry is a hero to the railroad workers. Flip through the book and find at least two examples of how he helps the people in this story.

In your own words, summarize why John Henry challenged the gnome and his machine to a race.

2

3

WHACK!

Why do you think the panel borders are so jagged here? How does it connect to the action in the story? (Turn back to pages 12–13 if you need help.)

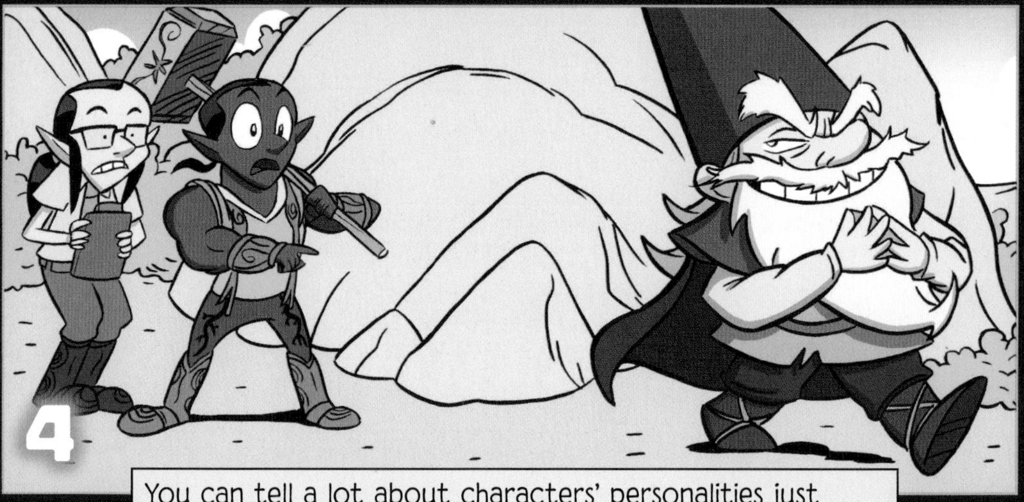
4

You can tell a lot about characters' personalities just from how the artist draws them. How would you describe Mr. Snotsworthy? What in the art makes you think that?

How do you think John Henry feels as he smashes through Witchfinger Mountain? Point to specific examples in the art and text to support your answer.

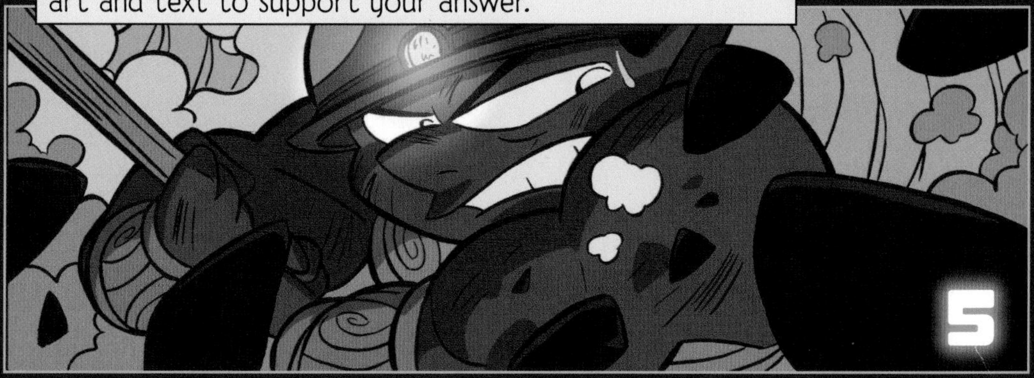
5

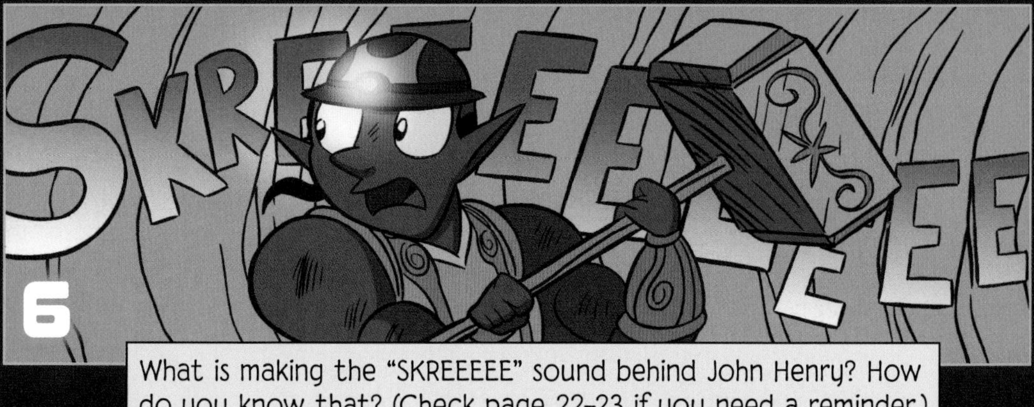
6

What is making the "SKREEEEE" sound behind John Henry? How do you know that? (Check page 22–23 if you need a reminder.)

AUTHOR

Benjamin Harper has worked as an editor at Lucasfilm LTD. and DC Comics. He currently lives in Los Angeles where he writes, watches monster movies, and hangs out with his cat Edith Bouvier Beale, III. His other books include the Bug Girl series, *Obsessed with Star Wars*, *Thank You, Superman!*, and *Hansel & Gretel & Zombies*.

ILLUSTRATOR

Alex Lopez became a professional illustrator and comic book artist in 2001, but he's been drawing ever since he can remember. Lopez's pieces have been published in many countries, including the USA, UK, Spain, France, Italy, Belgium, and Turkey. He's also worked on a wide variety of projects from illustrated books to video games to marketing . . . but what he loves most is making comics.

GLOSSARY

contest (KON-test)—an event in which people try to win by doing something better than others

cursed (KURSD)—under the power of an evil spell that causes bad things to happen

deserve (dih-ZURV)—to earn something through your actions or qualities

device (dih-VAYSS)—an object or machine made to do a specific job

elf (ELF)—a being from stories that looks like a small human with pointed ears and is sometimes described as having magical powers

explore (ik-SPLOR)—to go searching or looking around

foreman (FOHR-muhn)—the person in charge of a group of workers

gnome (NOHM)—a being from stories that often looks like a little old man and is described as living in the earth or guarding treasure

legendary (LEJ-uhn-der-ee)—famous for doing great things and talked about in stories

mine (MAHYN)—to dig up valuable materials that are underground

orc (ORK)—a monster from stories that is often described as ugly and violent

profit (PROF-it)—the money made after all the costs of running a business have been subtracted

TRULY LEGENDARY TALES

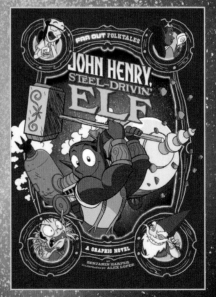

FAR OUT FOLKTALES

ONLY FROM capstone